Blackberry Bill

Blackberry Bill

Published by The Conrad Press in the United Kingdom 2018

Tel: +44(0)1227 472 874
www.theconradpress.com
info@theconradpress.com

ISBN 978-1-911546-37-5

Copyright © Ned Reardon, 2018

The moral right of Ned Reardon to be identified as author of this work has been asserted in accordance with the Copyright, Designs and Patents Act 1988.

All rights reserved.

Typesetting and Cover Design by:
Charlotte Mouncey, www.bookstyle.co.uk

The Conrad Press logo was designed by Maria Priestley.

Printed and bound in Great Britain
by Clays Ltd, Elcograf S.p.A.

Blackberry Bill

NED REARDON

In loving memory of 'Micky'

Chapter 1

Three days ago Tom Langley walked out of his life.
He packed a bag and hurried away from everything and everyone. Then he came here to this place; this shabby little room in the attic with its tiny roof window facing the sea, where he has sat and thought and dreamt of nothing but his earlier days back then... Back then, on those desolate marshes, when he was a boy.

Chapter 2

The boy who sat quietly and alone in the churchyard was ten years old. He gazed down at the fresh flowers, little orange ones this time, which somebody had placed upon his parents' grave. Yet another floral tribute. They had kept appearing mysteriously at the foot of their headstone for as long as he could remember. As always, he wondered who was responsible for them. A friend, possibly of his mother or father, or an unknown relative. It was a mystery he was determined to solve.

Interrupting his thoughts, a sudden gust of wind sailed briskly through the old elms, violently rustling the leaves. For a few moments the boy felt released from his quandary. He knew the sea was close by for it evoked a sound similar to the surf breaking upon a pebble shore. He adored the ocean and listened attentively until the breeze had run its course. Except for the cawing of a few rooks nearby, the deathly silence came once more, restoring a sense of foreboding amongst the forsaken graves. Alas, for the deceased, a sad and lonely permanence was ubiquitous, for here upon this hallowed earth past mourners had whittled to few and far between.

The boy now spent most of his free time here, sitting amongst the tombstones. And he just waited… and waited…

The vicar once told him that it is sometimes easier on the heartstrings never to have known one's parents rather than to painfully endure their loss during one's childhood. But the boy's heart ached to the contrary having grieved for them ever since he was able to comprehend his own unfortunate circumstances. He'd already found out that his parents had died during his infancy so he had never really known them. But he wished he'd been able to have seen them as they once were. As real people. Alive people.

For him, this would of course had just been a wonderful, miraculous whim but by the grace of God, if only granted for just one day of his lonely life, when he could have held their hands and felt the warmth of their parental love. An inconceivable day in the history of time when he'd be permitted to glance upon their mortal flesh, smell their scent, converse with them and oh how so lovely to have actually embraced them! But most of all to have been able to tell them how much he loved them both.

His eyes welled with emotion for the solemn truth was that he owned no memories of his deceased parents. Only visual fantasies are what comforted and sustained him. All he really possessed of them were their names graven on their tombstone.

Stark, cruel, heart-breaking letters etched out of the stonemason's cold slab which marked the remains of his entire family now lying dead and buried forever beneath the heavy white stone.

In Sacred Memory Of
Thomas Edwin Langley

> *Died 20thFebruary, 1958*
> *Also*
> *Isabella, Constance*
> *Loving wife of the above*
> *Died 20th February 1958*
> *R.I.P*

Nor had he ever seen any true likenesses of them for he'd been most profoundly informed by the local authorities, who were also now directly responsible for his welfare and upbringing, that there weren't any.

His parents, along with all of their worldly belongings, namely *The Marianne*, a wooden-hulled sailing barge moored at Milton creek awaiting cargo bound for the port of London, had ceased to exist following a disastrous fire that had broken out one dark winter's night this nine years past. The boy had no other relatives.

The vicar had also told him that as a baby he'd been rescued from that terrible blaze by some person or persons unknown. The boy had always rather liked to believe that it was probably his mother or father whom had performed the heroic deed when placing their precious baby boy safely ashore out of harm's way. However, nobody has ever been able to give him a true and honest account of what did actually occur on that tragic night.

Chapter 3

While the tears were still wet in his eyes, he heard a grumbly, rustic voice from beyond the church porch. 'Hey you there!'

The boy swung round slightly surprised but instantly resumed his former carefree manner after noticing that it was only Joseph, old Joseph Crow, come to work on digging some poor soul's grave.

'I say… you there!' repeated Joseph, 'Can't you hear me? What are you up to there, boy?'

Having no desire whatsoever to talk to this man, the boy ignored Joseph's hollering and remained reticent.

The boy knew Joseph well. Joseph always wore the same dirty clothes, a ragged cloth cap, a hole-ridden V neck jumper, a grimy brown blazer, formerly belonging to the vicar but now torn at the elbows, some corduroy breeches and a pair of hobnail boots thick with graveyard mud. More often than not, he would greet folk with an unkind growl and it was common knowledge that he much preferred his own company and so he was given a wide berth by all and sundry.

Before now the boy had often contemplated that come

the day when the grumpy old gravedigger finally died, who'd then dig a hole for Joseph, himself?

The boy also knew that Joseph had been this way for the past two decades following the loss of his own wife and child. Ever since that fatal, stormy night when they had drowned out in the estuary and he'd died in spirit, he had endeavoured to join them in that other world in spirit without actually taking his own life. Throughout his widower years, night after night he'd wallowed in self-pity, pickled his organs in liquor and refused the friendly counsel of anyone who tried to help him. Nowadays there wasn't a parishioner left upon the entire marsh that he could call a friend. His only solaces were his pipe and tobacco, the spirits of the night and his own bitterness.

The boy sometimes imagined that Joseph was controlled or tormented by some exterior being. The boy knew that Joseph was rarely happy. Mostly Joseph sighed with discontentment and cursed the world for all to hear. But there was the odd occasion when he might whistle a merry tune or chant a lively sea shanty.

'Oh, blow the man down, bullies, blow the man down!'

He'd swing his pick axe and strike the virgin earth.

'To me way-aye, blow the man down.'

Again and again he'd strike the ground.

'Oh, blow the man down, bullies, blow the man down!
Give me some time to blow the man down!'

Sometimes when Joseph hadn't noticed him in the churchyard, this was usually after the man had turned up a bit tipsy, the boy would hide behind the nearest convenient gravestone and secretly watch him at work. It amused the boy to listen to Joseph talking to himself, which he'd realised was more productive when the man was under the influence. When this happened he often teased the old misery by gently lobbing small stones down into the open grave on top of him. Joseph's head would then automatically pop up above the mounds of excavated dirt. He'd squint his bloodshot eyes and grumble something wicked under his breath before returning to his labours.

The boy would then toss another piece of gravel down into the hole and low and behold Joseph would surface once again, each time becoming more flustered and angry than the last and so on and so forth, the severity of his temper much depending on the volume of alcohol he'd consumed. But never once had Joseph cottoned on to the boy's amusing little game which he'd usually play six or seven times at tormenting him in this fashion before he'd eventually tire of it and let him be. Today however, he hadn't the appetite for playing tricks. Today he just felt sad.

'You there, you young tearaway…be off with you now!' Joseph bellowed, feeling much out of sorts and a little hung over as was usual. 'I'm warning you,' he went on, almost at the end of his tether and in no mood for pesky kids. 'If you don't clear off out of here I've a mind to smash your face in,' he threatened, 'You hear me?'

The boy could hear him perfectly well but couldn't care a hoot and therefore made no attempt to move, remaining unconcerned and obstinate.

'I'll smash your skull to smithereens with this'ere shovel I will,' promised Joseph, his head thumping with pain. 'Shift yourself I say!'

The boy wasn't going to leave just yet and stubbornly held his ground. In truth he'd no desire at this point of his childhood to die but had ultimately decided that if Joseph was to hold true to his word then so be it.

Infuriated by his indifference, Joseph's patience finally expired. He charged over to the boy compelled by his temporary insanity like a mad man possessed. Ranting and raving with his spade held aloft and his face glowing scarlet red, he appeared intent on carrying out his threats but then quite suddenly stopped dead in his tracks.

The boy had already risen to his feet and turned about to face the angry man full on. 'Go ahead then Mr Crow,' he said, shaking in fear but oddly at the same time remaining somewhat apathetic about the ultimatum the man had hurled at him. 'I don't care what you do… I don't even care if I die!' But the boy's grievous statement and apparent fearlessness had clearly unsettled Joseph. Never before had anyone stood up to him with such courage, least of all a ten-year-old boy. Allowing his shovel to drop to the ground, he stood lost for words and was uncertain of what to do next.

Meanwhile, the boy resumed his position before the sad grave and quietly shed a few tears for the people lying beneath his feet and one or two for himself as well. He was astounded by his own bravery and in later years would come to regard this event as the only time he'd ever really felt his life seriously at risk.

Joseph thought hard on the present matter of his violent behaviour and, unusually for him, began to worry about the repercussions. During a recent bout of drunkenness, he'd begun to experience very unpleasant visions, nasty and macabre: terrifying apparitions which had scared him practically to death and almost driven him half out of his mind.

His paranoia led him to believe that the snivelling kid before him could just as easily be one of those same ghastly spirits cleverly disguised as an innocent-looking child. *But old Joe Crow ain't to be hoodwinked this time around,* he thought slyly. Mindful of this, he suddenly felt the urge to quickly make amends for his ridiculous outburst. To turn things around as it were so as to dupe this scanty young devil into thinking that he was in fact his friend.

And so, following an interlude of uncomfortable silence, he began to apologise, something he hadn't done for many a year, albeit in an artful manner. 'I'm sorry I'd try to scare you young'n…truly I am…It's these headaches you see… And when I get one of 'em I usually see red and I lose my temper and then it gets me half crazy with rage, especially when I see strangers in my boneyard.'

The boy dried his eyes upon his sleeve but remained nonchalant. This man was just a bully, he thought. It'd been a long time since Joseph had felt obliged to swallow his pride and eat humble pie but now found himself willingly kneeling down beside the boy, attempting to coerce him into some friendly chinwag. 'Arrgh… it's a sad business though ain't it, lad?'

The boy gave no indication whatsoever of wanting to engage in a conversation with this man who he knew to be a drunkard. He just wished he'd go away and leave him alone.

'I remember these two,' said Joseph, desperate to appease the boy.

Finally the boy's ears began to twitch with interest.

'That day,' continued the crafty gravedigger, 'when I covered them over.'

The boy then looked fixedly at Joseph wanting to hear more.

'A very sad day it was because those folks were well liked and respected… I should think half the village was in attendance that day,' he said. 'And the church… well that must have been packed to the rafters I reckon.'

The boy made no comment and was reluctant to make friends but clung on to every word Joseph spoke.

'But this ain't no place for a young'n to be. A fine young man such as yourself shouldn't be wasting his valuable time in this'ere creepy old boneyard,' he continued to grovel, still grimacing with the throbbing pain in his head.

'Those are nice marigolds,' he remarked, reluctant to give up on the boy, 'pick'em yourself did you lad?'

'No sir,' replied the boy, softly.

'What's that?' returned Joseph, struggling to hear, 'what did you say lad?'

'I said, no sir it wasn't me,' repeated the boy, a little louder. The respect for his elders, irrespective of whom they may be, again presiding over his thoughts. 'Did you see who it was sir?' he added, out of curiosity.

Now that his persistence was finally beginning to take affect Joseph relaxed marginally, but frowned. 'Did I see who it were what?'

The boy pointed down at the grave. 'Did you happen to notice who it was that left these flowers here?'

'Nar, I ain't seen nobody today…excepting yourself of course.'

'Well, maybe yesterday then?'

'Nope…, oh tell a lie, I did spy that Blackberry lurking round here yesterday afternoon but it'd hardly be him, would it?'

The boy expressed a little vagueness. 'Do you mean

the man that lives out on the marshes, the one they call Blackberry Bill ?'

'Aye lad, that's the fella, but if you take my advice you should steer clear of him because I've even seen that dinlo in here at the dead of night… God knows what he gets up to!'

The boy had no intention of steering clear. He stood up and tucked his hands into his trouser pockets and began casually strolling over in the direction of the churchyard gates. Joseph then happened to notice a black, crow like bird perched on a nearby tombstone. It had been present all the time the boy was beside the grave.

'Come on then Jack…we must go home now,' said the boy, addressing the bird. 'Goodbye Mr Crow.'

'Aye lad,' returned Joseph, relieved to be finally rid of the boy's ghost who he had in his own misguided opinion, triumphantly tricked and therefore for once manages to avoid the spirit's wrath. He then removed his cap, scratched his scalp and shook his head to clear away the last effects of his excess drinking.

Astounded, he watched the bird flap and squawk and then fly thrice around the boy's head before finally settling upon its young master's shoulder where it stayed contentedly. Joseph ran his tongue across the outside of his dry lips and swore an oath that it'll never taste another tot of whisky. Before the noon, he was back over the threshold of The Three Hats public house and soon after found himself three sheets to the wind.

Chapter 4

A tall, strong, dark-eyed man strode determinedly across the graves. He'd been tucked out of sight at the far end of the churchyard, hidden within the shadows, waiting patiently for the boy with the bird and the alcoholic gravedigger to leave. Finally with the place all to himself, he stared down curiously at the Langley grave, appearing somewhat lost and uncertain of his intentions. Before turning about and heading back to the open marsh, the stranger glared suspiciously over at the upper sash windows of the orphanage adjacent and saw beyond the lace curtain the obscure form of a child's face staring back at him.

The boy knew he himself had some serious thinking to do. He thought long and hard about what Joseph had said and in particular the part about Blackberry Bill. He could not understand how this strange man may have been acquainted with his own parents and was dubious to the notion of it actually being him whom had left the flowers. However, anything was possible and indeed if it did turn out to be so then he wanted to know why.

Finding out wasn't going to be simple though. The boy knew that Blackberry Bill was a notorious recluse who lived like a lone wolf somewhere out on the marshes. This eccentric man was rarely seen but would sometimes suddenly turn up like a bad penny. On occasions when boys like himself, whom were happily playing football in the street using a chalked up goal on the outer side of the churchyard wall, would instinctively disperse and scramble up the nearest trees or bolt down alleyways. And when the girls, who were busy playing their hopscotch and french skipping games, would simultaneously emit high-pitched screams before scuttling off home to their mother's aprons with their pigtails and ribbons bobbing up and down.

Not a kind, friendly thought was ever wasted in his direction. Passersby hurriedly crossed over the road to evade his presence. Some snarled nastily whilst others spat onto the ground in disgust. Washerwomen, scrubbing door steps with wet hair in curlers and scarves, slammed their front doors and bolted him out. And old timers bent on sticks, lowered their trilbys and shied away, never a greeting exchanged. Shunned by the whole community, his appearances were fairly uncommon as the majority of his time was spent aimlessly wandering the marshes. As to what purpose, nobody had got the foggiest idea and so it remained.

The boy had often been told though that it was the local travellers whom had first nicknamed him 'Blackberry' on account of the purple scars or birth marks spread about his mouth and eyes which gave the illusion of blackberry juice stains. The gypsy elders, whom often sat around their campfires at night, frightened their offspring with midnight yarns about old Blackberry's curse. Apparently they'd forbidden their young to go anywhere within sight of this fellow for the stains on his face they claimed were in fact that of dried human blood. They said that he was an awfully hungry man who ate nothing but children and was particularly partial to gypsy kids. These of course tasted much nicer than gorger children, especially when he'd boiled them slowly in a big iron pot! As was their parent's intention, the terror-stricken gypsy children took heed of the unconditional rule and stayed well away.

The gypsies, whom also lived out on the windswept marshes at an unofficial campsite down by the saltwater creek, were certainly a God fearing, superstitious lot. Having formed an opinion about somebody it was indubitably set in stone, a stance from which they could never be swayed.

They had dealt with this lonesome character on one occasion only. This was when they'd indirectly bought his horse through a third party many years ago under a burglar's moon at an offer they couldn't refuse. As it turned out they were eventually forced to sell their bargain buy at a considerable loss on to an equestrian sanctuary believing the animal to be jinxed.

There exists a code of honour amongst all Romany people and although they had deemed the stranger a member of their own race they had also solemnly vowed never to trust him again. Effectively, he was disowned before having even made their acquaintance.

Chapter 5

The boy's orphanage, Greenporch, nestled content and docile within the spiritual shadow cast by an ancient church tower. Save the medieval village of Milton Regis, a cluster of Tudor and Elizabethan dwellings of oak beams with white washed plaster between on the hill close by and a few scattered farm barns, the children's home and the Norman church side by side stood alone, isolated and engulfed by marshland.

Greenporch was his home for he'd never known anywhere else. Mr and Mrs Saffron, his legal guardians whom the boy regularly referred to as the wise ones, could be fairly strict at times but on the whole he felt he was treated correctly. In fact, he'd always felt safe and secure, cared for and loved even. Fundamentally though, he'd also continuously felt something wanting in his life, something desperately missing which would have naturally dampened the fire in his belly and eradicated the constant ache of misery lodged like a thorn deep in the invisible membrane of his soul.

Altogether there were seven girls and six boys residing at the children's home, and for the majority of the time, got along nicely with one another. Chores were compulsory;

each child allotted daily tasks according to their own ability. But there was also always plenty of free time for the children to enjoy fun and games. They went on regular outings, trips to the seaside mostly, where they were spoiled with candy floss and sticks of coloured rock.

Annual fortnightly holidays to resorts like Broadstairs and Margate had become the norm where the children competed for the finest sandcastles and rode the Big Dipper roller coaster in Dreamland and fell hopelessly under the spells of the Great Zoltar, the fortune-teller resident in a glass kiosk in every penny arcade. The boy was grateful and felt a lot better off than most of his school friends whom had *real* families, some of which though had never been able to afford such luxuries. For this at least, he was thankful.

A vestige of light had appeared from beyond the horizon signifying the beginning of a brand new day. The dawn had arrived and soon his quest would begin. The boy waited patiently as the darkness gradually faded revealing before his eyes a vast sea of fog. Thick rolling layers of low lying mist spread out upon the marsh. Like great ocean waves, each desperately clinging to one another and refusing to bow down and die as the all-powerful sun began to rise. Staring out of his dormitory window, he felt as though he was incarcerated in the stone tower of a giant's castle in the midst of a magical kingdom way up above the highest clouds.

The boy was aching to explore this strange domain ruled solely by wart-skinned toads and fairy-dusted dragonflies. A mysterious land that appeared every morning beyond the glass pane if only to torment his strong sense of adventure. Whereas for the other children, these wetlands were most definitely out of bounds and strictly taboo. Eerie and dangerous it may have been, but the boy was determined to discover the secrets of this forbidden world.

So he'd resorted to lies and dishonesty, having given his solemn oath never to tread these sodden marshes alone. In parts, according to those who knew, they were treacherous. A quagmire, where boys of his own age had dared to venture and never returned. Disregarding their warnings, he yearned to uncover the mysteries cloaked by these dark and devilish marshes which constantly beckoned him through weird and wonderful dreams. Persistent shadows of the night continued to darken the dormitory but he durst not switch on the electric light. The boy's eyes slowly grew accustomed to the semi darkness and as quiet as a mouse, as not to disturb the other children sleeping, he got himself dressed for the big day ahead.

When he glanced up furtively at the brass oval framed portrait of Jesus Christ, adorned in a maroon velvet robe and hung high up on the plain white wall, the boy felt His studious eyes to be judgmental and critical. Penitent, he bowed his head in shame for having lied to the people whom cared for him but at the same time he also felt a dire need to be able to roam the marshes with impunity. He glanced up at the picture again and crossed himself praying to his protector, gentle Jesus on the cross, for His divine forgiveness just this once. With his rucksack and boots clasped tight to his chest, he tiptoed out of the room and down the stairs. Down in the kitchen he set his plan in motion, a ploy which he'd rehearsed many times in his mind. He'd lain in bed and fretted about the consequences should his scheme fail and now a pang of guilt jabbed at his conscience. He'd had to lie to his guardians, managing to convince them that he'd been invited to stay at the friend of his, a freckle-faced cheerful lad called Christopher Crispin, for the first few days of the school summer break.

So it was imperative that Christopher Crispin did not contact him during this period and he hoped and prayed that his pal wouldn't be seen either by the wise ones or indeed by any of his fellow protégées. He thought it unlikely though, Christopher Crispin being the timid, lonesome boy he was. With sunken eyes which had hardly slept a wink and greasy jet black hair, neatly cropped and combed in the style of a Hollywood vampire, he reminded him of little Eddie Wolfgang Munster out of the American hit TV show. He lived in the village on the hill in a first floor apartment situated above his father's funeral parlor and rarely played with other children. He hadn't any siblings for his amusement either but was awfully keen on books, especially those concerning steam locomotives and railways. Once before, he'd invited the boy home to proudly show off his model railway set. The layout was huge and occupied half of the attic space which much impressed the boy especially when he was allowed to operate the control mechanisms. He quite liked Christopher Crispin, even though every other kid at school blatantly shunned the sallow looking undertaker's boy.

Personally, the thing that troubled him the most about his friend was the place where he actually lived. The chapel of rest seriously gave him the heebie-jeebies and so did his creepy looking father who also owned an uncanny resemblance to the immortal Count Dracula and furthermore was locally thought of as a sanctimonious old so and so. The door to Mr Crispin's office was shaped like the lid of a coffin and attached to the coffin door was a shiny brass skull about the size of a ping-pong ball used as a door knocker. Needless to say the boy never went back there again.

The boy had already loaded his bag with a variety of items which he'd stowed away over the preceding few days, namely an empty lemonade bottle, which he now took the opportunity of refilling with orange squash, some biscuits, crisps and boiled sweets. In addition he'd packed a pocket compass, a blunt penknife, his magnifying glass and a turtle neck jumper in case the evenings should turn cold.

The clock on the wall said it was a quarter to six, much later than he realised. He had better hurry up, he thought. He didn't want to be delayed by the attentions of Mr and Mrs Stickles – the caretaker and the cook who were shortly due to arrive to rustle up everyone's breakfast. After quickly preparing himself a couple of his favourite cheese and piccalilli sandwiches, he proceeded to steal some of the fruit from the cook's bowl, rearranging the remainder to make the theft less conspicuous and hurriedly shoved it all into his rucksack. Quite unrepentant, he gently turned open the key shaped like a large F in the backdoor lock and slipped silently out into the dawn of a glorious Saturday morning. The sun had finally escaped the horizon and lit up the sky with bright orange and yellow ochre streaks, illuminating the great expanse.

Before his adventure to explore the forbidden and forbidding marshes could begin in earnest, he wanted first to visit his parent's grave. Dodging through a gap in the broken church gates, he navigated a path towards the grave through patches of thick mist that still clung low about the tombstones. This was the first time that he'd experienced the graveyard like this, so eerily silent and still that even the spiders sat upon their dewy cobwebs dare not flinch or the birds perched up in the wet trees to utter the slightest sound. But the boy held no fear and upon his arrival noticed with interest that there had been another posie of fresh flowers respectfully placed before their headstone.

After paying his own respects, he was suddenly filled with a powerful motivation to seek out the whereabouts of the strange hermit known as Blackberry Bill. He was determined to find out if indeed it was this man who'd placed the flowers here and of course the reason why. Perhaps this rascal *had* been a friend of his parent's, he reasoned. Or maybe they'd employed him to undertake some kind of marine work aboard their sailing barge. If either of these conjectures turned out to be true, then his chances of gaining some significant knowledge about his parents from this man would be greatly enhanced.

Trembling with anticipation, he dared to ponder further on a glimmer of hope flickering across his mind. The remote possibility of a photograph of his mother and father. He then asked himself, could this so called rogue possess such a thing? A beautiful print which would be more precious to him than his own life. Bursting with this new resolve and with the utmost zeal, he hurdled the churchyard wall like a racing greyhound, running the length of the farmer's dirt track through the apple and pear orchards and beyond into the beauty of the wilderness that was the Milton marshes.

Chapter 6

Nearing the end of a long trek across the marsh, he heard the screeching cries of hundreds of seagulls. He saw them soaring high above the council landfill dump down alongside the saltwater creek appearing almost like the burnt ashes of paper floating weightlessly above an enormous bonfire.

After scrambling up the grassy bank of the sea wall, he could smell salt in the air and was somewhat surprised as he turned around noticing the amount of ground he'd covered already. From this vantage point, he spied the entire length of the creek's meandering course from its head at Flushing Street at the edge of the town down to its mouth at Kemsley where it joins the Swale.

Here he also felt comforted by the sight of his church, prominent on the horizon whence he had come. The great tower of the Holy Trinity Church stood noble and sentinel as it has done since ancient times, overlooking and guarding the splendour of the wilderness which now surrounded him.

It was beginning to get very warm and he was annoyed with himself for forgetting to bring his straw hat. After a brief glance up at the rising sun, he understood with much dismay that he would soon need to find some shade somewhere if he wanted to avoid being burnt to a crisp. Nevertheless, for the time being he was content to rest here a while, stripping down to his breeches and quenching his thirst by eating one of the stolen apples.

The tide had receded to its lowest point exposing the creek's slippery innards glistening like wet liver. Mounds of dove grey mud which smelled obnoxious, as they did more often than not, of a sulphurous odour rather like rotten eggs. It was a smell he and his fellow Miltonians had long grown accustomed to and in truth hardly ever noticed anymore.

Moored at Murston Dock across the creek the boy saw a rusty old paddle steamer that seemed to have fallen into disrepair. Affixed near the bow of the boat there was a nameplate that said, 'PS Medway Queen'. He watched idly as the shipwrights, a band of proud and nostalgic enthusiast's intent on restoring her to her former glory, applied their trades.

This must be the ship that Mr Stickles had spoken of, he thought. The one that had saved his life during the war. Sometime ago the caretaker had relayed to him what he'd learnt of the vessel's plight and in addition given him a brief summary of its valiant history. He'd told him that this much loved steamer was part of Winston Churchill's 'little ships flotilla' used at the beginning of WWII, rescuing around 7,000 soldiers of the British Army stranded on the bombarded beaches of northern France. In 1939 she was also requisitioned to evacuate hundreds of children from Gravesend to East Anglia.

The boy took another long look at her and felt glad that this lovely old lady of the sea was soon to be given a new lease of life, which he also felt only fitting for a heroine of Dunkirk.

Sitting down in the long, sun bleached grass amongst the wild poppies and grasshoppers, he was able to breathe in the fresh air of the North Sea yonder for here was the perfect place he'd sought many times through his vivid imagination. He loved the ocean and often dreamt of pirates and scallywags and of Sinbad's wonderous adventures sailing the seven seas. His love of all things nautical was a trait he had inherited from his seafaring father, the sea already firmly established within his young blood. One day he mused, when he was rich and successful, he would buy his own boat and sail her all the way round the world.

Lying back beneath the heat of the relentless sun, he became totally immersed in a summery world of butterflies and bumble bees, buttercups and daisies and wearily fell into a comforting slumber.

He hears imaginary sea birds and smells salt and seaweed and even the fishes beneath the briny water. He feels as though he is really there, fearlessly sailing alone upon the crest of a gigantic ocean wave aboard nothing more substantial than a ramshackle raft using his patchwork eiderdown tied to a pole for a sail and an estate agent's FOR SALE signpost board, turned on its head as a rudder. Behind him, he feels the power of an inordinate wind driving him and the fragile craft towards the horizon. Relentlessly rolling onward to the sun rising in a vast, hollow sky that reaches to infinity.

Only a short while later he was suddenly woken up. Now firmly back in this world he felt bereft. Something troubling had disturbed his innocent daydream and dragged him back into the realm of reality. Fear pinpricked his senses as a dark shape began to emerge through the haze of his sleepy eyes. He saw a slovenly man standing along the hillock that it seemed was urinating into the creek. When he'd finished the man picked up what looked to the boy like an ordinary garden digging fork before trudging out on to the salt marshes.

Using the back of his hand to shield his eyes from the glare of the sun, he decided to take a stint at watching the stranger. The man had halted midway across the salt marsh where he'd begun to dig the ground. The boy couldn't fathom out what the man was actually up to but gradually began to realize that he was possibly burying something… Or someone? he quickly reconsidered, with a quiver of shivers traversing the length of his spine. He dared to prop himself up a little further in order to gain a clearer view.

The man was wearing a plain white shirt with a crimson neckerchief, dark brown breeches held up by a pair of braces and a pair of tan coloured leather boots. A tinker perhaps? pondered the boy. He had an idea that it was also the same person who he'd noticed only the other day, loitering suspiciously in the churchyard.

A little while later the man was stood knee deep in the trench he had just dug. Who was he? he fretted. And was he up to no good? Maybe this guy was indeed the stranger he sought but he couldn't be certain at this distance. If it is Blackberry Bill, he considered, how does a ten year old boy acquaint himself with such an odd ball character? He could be dangerous. He could be mad even. The boy erred on the side of caution deciding that it was probably wiser to bide his time. First he needed to be sure that it was the right fellow and to work out a safer way of making contact. Perspiring heavily, he stood up in readiness to leave and after studying the man further, was relieved to learn that there weren't any signs of dead bodies at least. Reluctantly, he crept away in the opposite direction.

Chapter 7

A quarter of a mile downstream he came alongside some sunken barges that had clearly been abandoned long ago and left to the mercy of the tide. Creeping closer, the shipwrecks began to appear like the bony skeletons of some gigantic sea creatures beached on a graveyard of mud. The rotting wooden keels and bulkhead frames, like the spines and rib cages of whales, were all that remained. Sad carcasses strewn all over the salt marshes. In the midst of all this decay however, lay the sunken wreck of an iron tugboat, its huge funnel half rusted away and leaning lopsided.

The boy had a fancy the vessel could afford him some temporary respite from the blistering heat. It had become far too hot and sticky for comfort, the air close and clammy and a struggle to breathe. He decided to tempt providence and give it a go, having already deduced it feasible to attain this objective by using the barge's rib frames as stepping stones and to this effect eventually boarded the craft with the help of incorporating a length of rickety driftwood used as a makeshift gangplank.

Up on the deck he was able to see as far as the final reach of Milton Creek where it linked up with the Swale. A small fleet of dinghy sailing boats were racing round the Isle of Sheppey with their multi-coloured sails leaning in unison into a westerly breeze. He felt a little envious for there wasn't even a breath of wind here and the heat had become intolerable. Heatwaves distorted the middle distance and the creek's underbelly of shiny grey mud appeared like overlapping slabs of molten silver reflecting under the scorching sun.

He closed his eyes for a few moments and imagined what it would be like out on the high Swale among the racing sailors. Cutting the waves in a boat of his own with the wind in his hair, salt in his lungs and the sea spray raining in his face. Aspiring to even dizzier heights, he promised himself that one day when he had come of age, he too would master the art of sailing and become the greatest yachtsman ever.

At the stern of the vessel there was an open hatchway. He edged towards it cautiously avoiding the parts of the deck which had severely corroded, paper thin in patches. Balanced awkwardly above the hole, he peered down into the dark space below and was soon convinced that it was the chamber that housed the tug's anchor after noticing part of a coiled metal chain. When descending the iron ladder, he instantly felt the benefit of a sudden drop in temperature and after crawling on top of the rusty chains, saw that there was just enough room to squeeze himself beyond the daylight.

Cramped below deck it was dark and dank and eerily silent but a welcome relief from the oppressive heat. He felt exhausted and again his mind began to tire. Could one of the wrecks lying on the mud have been the '*Marianne*' barge? he asked himself. Could this be the place where his mother and father had perished?

He was then startled by a noise above which caused him to shrink back further into the darkness. Instantly he understood he was cornered. But then, to his utter relief, he noticed that it was only a bird that had hopped onto the rim of the hatch. It stayed there for a while preening itself. At first he wondered if it was *Jack,* escaped from his aviary, but when he glanced up he was met by the uneasy sight of a lone magpie gawking down at him. The boy stared up at the bird into its black beady eyes. 'One for sorrow,' he uttered, 'two for joy.' He waited for the second magpie, hoping. But the bird never came. Soon he was fast asleep.

Beyond the thinning mist as the great blue wave nears the end of the world headed towards the sky that is no more, the boy holds steady his nerve. The time comes soon enough when, knowingly, he looks sharply astern. In that very moment, the boy and his raft are hurtled forth into the black, star-studded ocean of space and he watches, with the saddest of hearts, the rapid white water far beneath him draining from every sea on the planet as it floods over the edge of the earth and disappears forever into the abyss.

But all is not lost. He is afloat once more. Gently adrift upon an invisible sea of peace and calm amid a spectacular new world, silent and unfurled. Now he weighs anchor and sets sail, charting a straight course towards the great vortex suspended in perpetuity between the celestial realms of past and future. Be patient my beloved mother and father, he cries out into the dark void. I am coming now. And thus begins his incredible journey across the heavenly universe to the Kingdom of the Lord.

Following his nap the boy awoke feeling invigorated and relaxed, cooled and calmed. No longer did he fret about the possibility of Christopher Crispin inadvertently giving the game away. Or about what his guardians might have to say to him when he had a mind to return to Greenporch. *What will be will be,* he thought. He would deal with their reprimands when the time came. This adventure, as far as he was concerned, had only just begun.

However, this pleasant sense of exhilaration and exuberance had deflated somewhat soon after vacating his convenient fox hole. Smothered in rust particles, he was aghast with the sudden realisation that he was in deep trouble. The tide had long turned and it seemed that he was now in serious danger of becoming trapped, cut off by the incoming sea water. With not a moment to spare, he clambered his way back down the gangplank with his thoughts racing in panic. The timbers he'd used earlier as convenient stepping stones were now submerged under the muddy water. Not to any great extent but the problem was that they had become completely invisible. He had no choice, the boy realised, other than to estimate at their proximity and hope for the best. Which meant of course getting his feet wet but needs must, he supposed.

Initially he coped, getting a good foothold on the solid framework and at about half way back all was well. At this stage he'd also managed to sling his rucksack over on to the sea wall. Now he could count some of his blessings for at least his supplies were safe and dry. The boy though was not so fortunate having misjudged a timber two steps later causing him to trip head first into the water. With some awkwardness, he gradually squelched his way back out of the creek drenched from head to toe in a foul smelling cocktail of grey mud and milky coloured slime. Spitting out the dregs of the filthy brackish water he cursed his rotten luck.

He was furious; a bath at this early stage of his escapade had definitely not been on his agenda.

The church, away on the horizon and its surrounding wood, grabbed his attention momentarily. He knew perfectly well that hidden just beyond the old elm and sycamore trees was Greenporch, his home where he had been forewarned by the wise ones, sat in their salubrious surroundings, never to come here alone. As he stood there stooped with his hair and skin caked in the disgusting, blancmangey mud, he could literally hear their taunts and jibes and imagine them scolding him at the forefront of his mind, wagging their fingers righteously.

Annoyed with his own foolishness, he plugged up his muddy ears with his muddy fingers and refused to accept their disparaging remarks.

The mud on his skin was drying fast and was beginning to feel prickly and uncomfortable as though alive with parasites. Hastily, he skimmed off as much as he could, using his bare fingertips but the situation was hopeless. He could hardly bear the smell of himself, the mud was repulsive and stank to high heaven. He felt dejected, upset and irritated with himself for having fallen into the creek but for now the urgency of a bath had become a more pressing matter. Now it seemed he had to return home with his tail firmly between his legs and having had his expectations knocked down a peg or two, he thought about what lay ahead. *Whatever will be, will be!*

Chapter 8

Trudging back across the hinterland despondently and his head hung low, he was suddenly halted in his tracks by the sight of something mesmerizing. He found himself staring at a clump of woodland that seemed almost to be afloat on a great yellow sea. It was located in the centre of a vast cornfield, which surprisingly, he hadn't noticed earlier on his way down to the creek. He was sweating prolifically and his skin itched terribly. Commonsense told him that he should continue on his homeward journey as fast as he could but try as he may, he could not avert his attention away from the mysterious looking island.

Then, overwhelmed by some crazy, whimsical impulse, whilst at the same time emitting a high-pitched scream imitating Tarzan's jungle cry, he leapt down into the corn. He couldn't see the island at all now and was amazed at how he'd disappeared bodily below the tall stalks. However, he still felt confident he'd find his way after retrieving the pocket compass from his rucksack.

It didn't take him very long to reach the isle where he followed the perimeter around the poplar trees until he discovered a sufficient gap in the dense gorse wide enough for him to crawl through.

When he got beyond the rough brambles and stinging nettles, his eyeballs almost popped out of their sockets as he came before a large pond, abounding with algae and covered in water lilies. He was stood gaping at the fresh water pool sunk in the midst of an explosion of colour more striking than a coral reef, ringed by copious amounts of flowering shrubs, alluring exotic plants and overhung by trees drooping in full bloom. In the succeeding months he would learn what they were, fuchsias, cedars and magnolias, to name but a few. Even the sheen upon the water's surface was radiant with every colour of the rainbow. The boy had to pinch himself for he wasn't quite sure if he hadn't just stumbled into somebody else's dream. The whole place was aglow with sublime beauty, a picturesque utopia beyond his wildest imagination, inhabited by fat frogs, nimble newts and scaly lizards. Through wide open, innocent eyes which struggled to believe, he saw a mystical, amphibious world patrolled by magnificently coloured dragonflies darting adeptly from one bulrush to another above an army of pond skaters and lesser water boatmen.

Without warning something then began to emerge from the water causing the startled boy to instinctively hit the deck. Fearful once again, his heart began to beat furiously and terror quickly seized hold of all of his senses. Although it'd only been a fleeting glimpse, he'd noticed that the man was naked but more alarmingly felt certain that it was also the same person he'd seen earlier, burying something out on the salt marsh. The man must have been swimming underwater and had presumably resurfaced for air. In that split second the boy had also observed some very distinguishing marks around both his eyes and mouth. There was no doubt in his mind now that the bather was indeed the man that the villagers called 'Blackberry Bill'. The grotesque scaring he'd noticed was also prominent on the man's chest and on the front side of his legs like he was suffering with some type of skin affliction.

The boy started to panic. Had the man seen him? Was he creeping quietly towards him this very moment? Almost choking on his own fear he dared not to twitch a muscle. Too afraid to look up, too afraid to scratch at his itchy skin, too afraid to breathe even, he thought about the portrait of Jesus Christ and prayed to Him now for protection. He laid trembling and also thought about the gypsy's tale. Was he about to be throttled to death and eaten? He squeezed his eyes shut, swallowed his fear and listened with bated breath for all his life was worth.

Nothing. Not a murmur. Deafening silence broken only by the thudding pulse of his own heartbeat. No sounds of splashing water. No huffing and puffing. Peace and calm had returned save for the sound of a cuckoo, cuckooing somewhere close by. Maybe the man had gone? He desperately hoped so. Raw fear niggled his nerves but it was now or never. He had to try and make a dash for it. Three… Two….One and he was up in readiness to flee. There was nobody there. He was quite alone.

Not quite trusting his own eyes he scanned his immediate surroundings for any sign of the man's presence. There wasn't any. Not a trace of the strange man or his clothing were evident. He'd even begun to doubt his own sanity. Maybe he hadn't really seen him at all. A mirage perhaps? Too much exposure to the sun. Only now was he able to drop his shoulders and exhale a long sigh of relief.

After finally regaining his breath his confidence slowly returned, enough so for him to strip down to his underwear and step gingerly into the pool. Initially, the pond water had felt quite tepid but as he paddled out he noticed how much cooler it became. In the centre it was also deep enough to swim around in but first he had to wash every bit of dried dirt away from his sticky hair and grimy sunburned hide.

Floating on his back, gazing up through the leafy trees at the empty blue sky, his anxiety mellowed into a form of contentness. He couldn't quite believe his luck, a Garden of Eden right bang in the middle of nowhere. He swore to himself never to breathe a word of its existence for here he felt completely free, overwhelmed by a pleasant sense of euphoria. He wanted this place all to himself and resented the fact that Blackberry Bill was obviously aware of it too. He wondered if anyone else did? Most likely not. Blackberry Bill and himself and possibly old farmer Pat, the land owner were probably the only people, he surmised, whom had ever relished its tranquillity.

Satisfied that he was now completely clean he stood at the water's edge dripping wet, realising rather stupidly that he hadn't anything to dry himself off with. Craning his head up at the blazing sun, he felt sure that it would complete the task for him. He set about the other job of rinsing out his dirty clothes including his footwear and hung the whole lot willy-nilly on some nearby bushes. He'd be nice and dry in no time at all and as for his boots and clothes, they would dry eventually. Alongside the weeping willow, naked and sopping wet, he sat down on the trunk of a fallen tree, coated yellow-green with lichen and moss and waited patiently for the sun to do its work.

Negotiating those slippery timbers had been more than

he'd bargained for but it mattered little to him now. He'd begun to fend for himself precociously and he considered this a positive thing. In fact he couldn't recall ever feeling quite this happy. Here alone on the marsh, he felt as though he was slowly becoming a man and having erased all memory of his deceptions was now more resolute than ever.

In that moment, he'd even begun to muse over the concept of moving there for good, weighing up the practicalities of such an undertaking. For instance, the problem of having somewhere warm and dry to sleep was easily solved if he bought himself a small, second hand tent at the jumble sale with the pocket money he'd saved already. He'd live by eating the fish that he'd catch himself and learn to hunt rabbits and maybe grow some vegetables too. He thought he could be just like Robinson Crusoe, the resourceful castaway marooned on an island and nobody would ever know he was there... But then, he sighed, wouldn't he be sorely missed back at Greenporch? And in particular by his dear friend Jack.

Chapter 9

Listening to the songbirds had reminded the boy of his pet jackdaw which he'd found when only a fledgling. He'd noticed the bird balancing precariously on top of his parent's headstone. Flapping its tiny, undeveloped wings in some obvious distress, he could only assume that the poor creature had somehow fallen from its nest or maybe even crashed into the tombstone on its maiden flight.

More worryingly, he'd also noticed a mangy-looking ginger tomcat prowling nearby who he suspected was planning to eat the baby bird for his breakfast. Of course he'd felt compelled to deprive the hungry cat of his free meal, (not that he'd anything against cats), shooing it far away before rescuing the injured jackdaw. He'd instantly named the pitiful, helpless thing 'Jack' and concerned for the animal's welfare, decided to smuggle him into Greenporch where he secretly sustained the bird on tiny worms and pieces of stale bread soaked in sour milk.

The boy had had to beg the wise ones to keep Jack after his little secret had been discovered only a few days later. They'd refused outright, claiming that it wasn't ethical and that it was basically cruel to keep a wild animal domestically. Mr

Stickles, the home's gardener and general caretaker however, was of the opinion that the bird had unfortunately damaged a wing which needed a little more time to heal. Following a reconsideration of the bird's predicament, he was then granted temporary permission to retain the animal during its time of convalescing. Nursing the bird back to full health had become a very laborious job for the boy and by the time he'd actually made a full recovery Jack had already grown into his prime, his feathers shiny and as black as coal.

The boy had tried his utmost to introduce his foundling back into the wild where he truly belonged, adopting all sorts of crafty procedures in order to outwit the bird but alas, failing miserably at every attempt. Jack was far too clever by half and had stubbornly made up his own mind that Greenporch was his home now and that was the way it was going to stay! To be perfectly honest nobody at the orphanage, including Mr and Mrs Saffron, had really wished him to leave anyway for he had become quite a celebrity. It so transpired that the boy was allowed to keep the jackdaw as his pet for good.

Mr Stickles kindly constructed a permanent aviary out of bits of driftwood and chicken wire. The cage was meant only to protect the bird from natural predators such as stray cats and foxes and not to imprison him. The caretaker had ingeniously incorporated a unique *Jacksize* doorway which meant the bird was free to come and go as he so desired.

The bird had become excellent company for the boy and so amusing too, a prodigy in fact. More often than not, following some of its impish antics, it'd have the most hardened of dispositions rolling around in fits of laughter. On one such occasion, when the tortoise was out on the summer lawn, the jackdaw had walked up to it rather inquisitively fearlessly cocking its head from side to side trying to figure out exactly what the strange looking creature was. It wasn't too long before Jack had developed a practical use in his new found friend by hopping up on to the tortoise's shell and hitching a free ride around the garden whenever it took his fancy.

Much of the time the jackdaw stayed on its best behaviour which was attributed somewhat to its wonderful temperament and human-like characteristics. Even so, like its human counterparts, the bird would occasionally play up, taking it upon himself to fly up to an open window where he would casually remove various items of jewellery from the girl's dormitory, much to their repeated annoyance. Fortunately for Jack, the boy without fail would rush to his best friend's defence, disclaiming their accusations of theft and nuisance and assuring them that the intelligent creature had merely borrowed their bangles and trinkets as toys to play with. The girls were always reunited with their property and ultimately the bird was always forgiven.

Chapter 10

When he reached into his rucksack to take a swig of his orange squash, he suddenly remembered the magnifying glass. It was just the thing he needed right now and within a few minutes, using the sun's rays in conjunction with the glass, he succeeded in igniting a flame for a small fire of dry twigs and reeds. He was rather pleased with himself for what he'd achieved but at the same time was anxious that perhaps the smoke from his fire could bring some unwanted attention to his whereabouts, especially with regard to the naked swimmer he'd seen earlier. Nevertheless, it was a risk he had to take. The heat had already dried his skin and so now with the aid of the fire he proceeded to dry off every article of his wet clothing.

In what seemed to be no time at all, he was fully dressed again in dry clothes and ready to carry on with his adventure. Staring at the pond he felt truly thankful for it. A Godsend. He was clean and dry, albeit reeking of wood smoke and somewhat wiser about the comings and goings of the tide, but basically there was now nothing stopping him from continuing on as before.

Like the sun hat he'd left behind, he also began to regret

not having fetched his fishing rod and tackle. There might have been some carp or bream up for grabs, he sighed. But then again, he thought, what was the use of his fishing gear without maggots for bait? He stamped out the dying embers of the fire and departed the secret island paradise feeling happy and a little proud of himself for having overcome his first taste of adversity.

Cast adrift amidst a perpetual summer's day his quest had resumed. Rambling across the wetlands, climbing over stiles, leaping dykes and ditches he felt alive with an even greater sense of engagement. For the first time in his life he was rich with liberty and felt like the whole beautiful world belonged to him alone.

Chapter 11

The boy had spent the afternoon walking the sea wall all the way round to the King's Ferry bridge which connected the mainland to the Isle of Sheppey, enjoying some wonderful views of the Swale and its pastoral marshes. Knowing it was prohibited to go there he'd wanted to find out if it was possible to see (which unfortunately it wasn't) from the advantageous position of the river crossing, an uninhabited strip of land known as Dead Man's Island which lies low in the throat of the Swale opposite Queenborough Harbour. He wanted to find out a bit more about this rather unusual place following an interesting conversation he'd overheard recently in the Hasty Tasty café. The ex-matelots from the houseboats down on the creek were chatting to some fellow boat dwellers from Faversham creek and had stated that two hundred years ago the small island was used solely as a burial ground for deceased sailors from infected ships and also for convicts who died on the prison hulks anchored out in the estuary.

They'd also implied the existence of a strange, haunting presence thought to be the spirits of a hundred restless souls. Their rotting coffins and skeletons can now be seen poking out of the muddy ground where the sea has long eroded the land. The boy could only imagine it to be a very sad and lonely place upon which nothing moves except perhaps occasionally the bones themselves.

The sun, already long into its reluctant descent, was gradually drawing the long day to a close. Evening had slowly crept up behind him but now content to have gained his bearings, he chose to make his way back to Milton Creek. A zephyr began to stir and breeze gently through the boy's hair. This was his amazing new world. As far as his eyes could see was his to roam and explore.

Again he was soothed by the formidable sight of the church silhouetted against a reddening skyline. According to the hearsay of an old lady he'd once chatted to inside the church, when he had gone there to light a candle for his parents, she had referred to it as the 'Cathedral-in-the-Marsh' and had suggested that it is arguably one of the proposed sites Saint Augustine had had in mind for his church when he first arrived in Britain on the shore nearby, as a missionary sent by Pope Gregory the Great in 597AD.

The boy was also aware of a rumour that it concealed a tunnel underneath its graveyard which leads supposedly all the way up to the manor house in the village on the hill. They'd said that the original purpose of this underground passage was the means for the good folk of Milton to escape foreign invaders, marauding pirates and the likes whom had sailed in stealth upstream with murderous intentions and with a mind to ransack, pillage and rape. He'd often searched for the legendary tunnel's entrance himself but like others always to no avail.

He stared into the far distance at the church's enormous tower and battlements built of ancient sacred flint and drew a kind of spiritual strength from it. At ten years old he may have only been a splinter of a man but at that very moment of his boyhood he'd felt the worth of ten courageous men.

In the opposite direction he could see a thin plume of blue smoke gently rising from beyond the washbacks where the old brickworks used to be. Already conversant of the knowledge that Blackberry Bill was living out that way somewhere, he began to deliberate. Should he play safe and return to the secret wood? Or should he throw his caution to the wind and try to seek him out now? He chose the latter for now he was in the right frame of mind, feeling truly invincible. With a couple hours of daylight still remaining and suddenly possessed with the courage of a lion, he turned and headed for the washbacks with a definite spring in his step.

Chapter 12

Nowadays the washbacks are barely visible, having overgrown with grass and bramble and forsaken long ago, on this side of the creek, by a once busy and thriving brick making industry. Basically they were man-made earth hillocks not unlike the sea defenses seen around the North Kent shores, except these were shaped into rectangular enclosures. For example, some were about the size of a standard tennis court. The hillocks that formed the washbacks stood around 3 metres high by near 4 metres wide. Elevated brick and earth mounds that encaptured pools or reservoirs of a mixture of brick earth and chalk slurry which had been 'washed' of any impurities such as stones, pebbles and shell and then left to settle. The end result culminating in a pliable, pug like substance that was then cut away from the settling pond and transported to the brick sheds for shaping and moulding into standard building bricks and then finally stacked onto hacks for drying and into the kiln for burning.

The boy was now stood in the crux of one of these abandoned washbacks whence he had traced the source of the rising smoke. It was coming from a small tubular metal chimney poking up through the roof of an old-fashioned bowtop vardo. A horse-drawn gypsy caravan, embellished with elaborate wood carvings and delicate paintwork. He'd been told already that Blackberry Bill had pulled up on these marshes some years back, sold his horse to the local travellers and had lived like a recluse ever since.

The front end of the caravan comprised a stable type door of which the top half happened to be extended open. He could hear someone whistling and it was coming from inside the vardo. After quickly backpedaling, he crouched down and concealed himself behind an elderberry tree growing at the entrance to the washback.

One thing that immediately struck the boy was how quiet it was here. Such a blissful place in which to live. Soon he would come to learn the names of everything that grew there. Ever-present, thriving in and amongst the sedge and wild grasses were poppies and knapweed, common valerian, meadowsweet and yellow rattle and flourishing all along the inside of the banks were lots of gangly hollyhocks and sunflowers. There was also an allotment loaded with an array of vegetables. Leafy runner bean plants sprouting up around cane poles, overshadowing rows of rampant cauliflowers, lettuces and cabbages. There was a rhubarb patch, lush and overgrown and even some strawberries ripening under fine netting.

Turning his attention to the man's possessions, he conducted a visual survey of everything before him. He was interested specifically in anything resembling a big iron pot but thankfully there was nothing of the sort. Just outside the caravan lying on some patchy grass, his busy eyes homed in on a tin bath which was three parts full of dirty brown water. Over the bath stood an oblong table stacked high with an assortment of stone jars and glass bottles. It was the same sort of stuff that he'd already noticed littered all over the marshes except these particular ceramics weren't broken. Everywhere he looked there were empty bottles and jars stood in rows, different shapes and sizes and coloured green, amber and blue. Also spread around on the ground were heaps of stone flasks and china pots. He wondered why on earth did the man want to keep so many of these dirty old pots? What use were they now? After all it was only the unwanted trash the Londoners had discarded decades ago.

At around the turn of the century, a time when the brick making industry of the town would have been operating at full capacity, the brickmakers in particular transported the bulk of their manufactured goods by way of the working barge boats. Most of which headed up the Swale and around into the Thames estuary before sailing up river straight for the capital. On their return voyages they'd fetch back thousands of tonnes of London refuse, dust and ashes. Packaging in those days consisted mainly of porcelain and earthenware vessels, clay flasks and glassware. This material, once rejected, gradually found its way out of London and was discharged finally around the little ports of the eastern counties. A great deal of this stuff came to Milton docks where it was then unloaded into hand barrows and horse carts and dumped all over the marshland both sides of the creek. Next it was then buried with a thin layer of earth and forgotten for evermore. Now it would appear, thought the boy, that this strange man known as Blackberry Bill was intent on digging it all back up again.

He turned around and gazed back across the marshes at all the pits which the man had already produced. Scores of holes everywhere, all with heaps of loose soil and broken pottery lying beside each abandoned excavation. Some of the holes were mere ruts but some were as large as empty graves. He calculated that it must have taken the man many years to have dug them all. Whatever had motivated him to do such a foolish thing? he wondered. To waste his life digging up worthless rubbish. Blackberry Bill was a man who dug up pots. A potdigger. And the boy likened him to a human mole.

All of a sudden somebody appeared at the caravan door. It was the same tall, dark and strong looking man that he'd seen out on the sea wall and at the wooded isle. It *was* Blackberry Bill. The boy kept well back out of sight but continued to secretly observe the gypsy man with a mixture of fear and excitement whizzing around his abdomen.

The man climbed down the vardo steps, held up both arms aloft and groaned a long satisfying yawn. Now that the boy had managed to get this close the gypsy's facial disfigurement was easily more noticeable. But because of the severe blemishes it was difficult for him to judge the man's age which he guessed could have been anywhere between his early twenties and mid-thirties. He certainly seemed fit and agile as he proceeded to drag two heavy looking hessian sacks from the side of the steps over to the tin bath.

The boy then recoiled in disgust. He suddenly thought, what if the gypsies' implication about him being a cannibal was really true? He began to worry about what might be in the sacks. Was he about to witness some dreadful abomination? He could barely watch, his heart pounding in anticipation.

When the man untied one of the sacks the boy gasped and closed his eyes tight until curiosity had forced them back open again only moments later. He hadn't noticed that he'd been holding his breath and couldn't help but exhale a long sigh of relief after he saw the man innocently pull out a couple of dirty bottles. These he set about washing one at a time in the brown water before examining each item, checking for faults such as cracks or chips in the glass which if discovered were promptly disposed of by chucking them onto a separate broken pile. He repeated this task over and over again until the bag was completely empty. The second sack turned out to contain clay pots which were attended to in the same fashion as before. There was more to these funny old pots then met the eye, thought the boy. But no matter how hard he strained his brains he was unable to decipher any logical reason why the man should pay them so much attention.

The boy leapt back behind the tree when the working man just happened to glance over in his direction. Tucked out of sight once more, he couldn't be certain if he'd been tumbled or not but this time he had no intention of hanging around to find out. With body and limbs tingling with nerves, he picked up his trembling legs and shot off across the open marsh like a hunted coursing hare, trying his utmost to avoid falling down any of the potdigger's numerous holes.

When he felt reasonably sure it was safe to rest he came to a sudden halt and gasping for breath, bent over to nurse a stitch in his side. Hands on knees and puffing and panting, he slowly turned his head around and was surprised to learn that the man hadn't made the slightest attempt to pursue him. Instead he was stood quite still on the crown of the washback, his lanky frame prominent against the darkening sky. Arms folded, the gypsy wasn't the least bit perturbed by his recent intruder but was keen to observe the boy's progress across the marsh with a nosey parker's curiosity until he'd faded into the dusk.

Even though the boy was glad that he'd finally found the gypsy's home, he also felt a tad disappointed with himself for having refrained from his original purpose. But to be perfectly honest his pluck had deserted him and he'd become very afraid, shuddering at the thought of clashing with this unpredictable man who'd appeared aloof and unapproachable. So the boy cherished no desire at this point of his audacious exploit to go against the grain of his intuition but he also knew that soon, if he was ever going to achieve his goal, he would have to overcome this fear.

Chapter 13

An abundance of grazing wild rabbits suddenly bolted for the safety of their burrows and a young stoat fleeing for cover shot by his legs. He looked up and saw the kestrel soaring high above. The majestic hunter fluttered and hovered effortlessly in the burnt sky, poised to strike its prey below. An unsuspecting field mouse or a vole perhaps, he thought. Then with both stealth and speed the falcon swooped down into the long grass, reappearing a moment later with the doomed furry rodent clasped tight beneath its distinctive hooked bill.

Scampering his way back across the grassy plain, tinderbox dry and alive with the sound of roosting bird wildlife, he listened in particular to the sporadic cries of the curlew sandpipers. Their hypnotic calls calmed him and helped to clear his mind. He'd been thinking about what he should do next and finally decided it prudent to spend his first night on the secret wooded island. He'd be safe enough there and if he hurried there was still time enough in which to construct himself some sort of temporary shelter.

It was getting late and he was feeling tired and hungry. He thought about the other orphans back at Greenporch, whom would've all by now scoffed down their lemon sponge and custard desserts, it being a Saturday. And worse still, tomorrow the lucky beggars would have the pleasure of a roast dinner to look forward to. His stomach grumbled with envy and just for a minute or two, whilst licking his lips, he'd even considered what excuses he could muster if he should decide to pack it all in and run all the way home. The front door would probably be locked by now, he thought. Even so he could always sneak back in down through the coal hole. Feeling a little ashamed for allowing his resolve to have weakened, he sucked on the last piece of his aniseed twist and shook the notion away. At least he'd become aware of this and in some strange way this lapse had helped to fortify his overall determination to succeed. To see this thing through and finish what he'd started. No, I'm not a quitter, he quickly reconsidered. I shan't give in that easily!

On reaching the wood these feelings of morose had all but diminished and to the contrary his spirits actually lifted after he'd discovered a few smouldering embers of his original fire. Soon after he was enjoying the luxury of another small fire burning which would give him warmth and security throughout the night. He promised himself to keep a vigil over the flames ensuring that they never went out and making use of his penknife, prepared another bundle of dry kindling for use later on.

Overhead the colours in the evening sky were truly spectacular. Like clouds on fire, an inferno of scarlet and vermillion compressed by the encroaching twilight. '*Red sky at night, shepherd's delight*' He assumed tomorrow would be as hot as today. In keeping with this theory he didn't believe it would rain anytime soon but he'd learnt never to be complacent with regard to the weather, especially on these North Kent marshes. Just to be on the safe side he built himself a flimsy but perfectly adequate shelter, a wig-wam type camp using branches and doc leaves. For his supper he ate his biscuits and crisps and toasted the cheese and piccalilli sandwiches that he'd stowed away, using a stick as a prong. Afterwards, he piggishly ate all of his fruit as well. Now he had no food left whatsoever.

As the day gently surrendered to the night, smothering the trees under the blanket of its silent mystery, the boy began to feel a touch apprehensive. He'd never once been afraid of his own company and for the most part welcomed solitude. But the darkness had arrived and this would be the first time that he'd ever slept out under the stars. Never before had he felt quite so alone.

The fire crackled and spat, owls hooted and bats flapped and tiny invisible creatures scurried across the ground and along with a multitude of unexplainable noises, he'd been spooked out of his goose pimpled skin from time to time. In between, he'd gazed up in awe at the shooting star propelled across the night sky and saw the Great Bear Constellation Ursa Major and Polaris, the North Pole star, and he knew that far beyond those trillions of twinkling bright eyes was the beginning of heaven and God the Almighty and forever and ever.

Sat on the threshold of his tenuous tepee camp with everything awash in the shine of the full moon, he said hello to its doppelganger appearing on the glass like surface of the pond. He thought it was incredible that NASA were planning on sending Man there next year via Apollo 11. Their astronauts were scheduled to step foot on the lunar planet marking the first major leg of mankind's journey into the unknown through eternal space.

On the grand scale of things, he suddenly felt quite meaningless and insignificant like a tiny speck of human dust. But he was just as important as anything else, he reassured himself. There was a purpose to his own existence like there was a reason for everything. Tending to lean optimistically, he'd always believed that beyond the gloom there was hope like there was behind every cloud a silver lining. Finally, he accepted the darkness and mother nature's wilderness and the pleasant sense of freedom which had come all about him and no longer did he feel afraid.

It is dark. Very dark. Darker than he'd ever known the night to be. Yet, strange as it may sound, he can plainly see the distinctive form of a huge man drifting in and out of the mist. At least 10 feet tall, hooded and cloaked in black and eclipsing a strange fluorescent glow, the faceless phantom stands perfectly still.

'Are you Death?' asks the boy.

The thing does not reply but it is there. He can hear it breathing, struggling for air as though its throat and chest are heavily congested with snot and mucus.

'Have you come for me?' pursues the boy.

Following a short spell of reckoning it replies slowly through rattling phlegm. 'No, I've not come for thee, but for another.'

'Who?' Pleads the boy, 'Who have you come for?'

'That is not for you to know.' It concludes, spitting globules of yellowish-brown bile. Then, turning its back on the boy, it looks towards the far end of the foggy marshes where a tiny beacon of light has suddenly appeared.

The boy thinks that it's perhaps a lighted candle in somebody's window. Once again he asks, 'Who have you come for Mr Death?'

'Go home young whippersnapper!' It retorts, clearly irritated by the boy's inquisition. *'Now is not your time…But rest assured, one day I'll come back for you too!'* And then it almost chokes, laughing hysterically.

The boy inches back and watches apprehensively as the spectre glides across the long, wet grass towards the speck of light burning in the village on the hill. He prays for the candle's owner and hopes that he or she has at least lived a long and purposeful life. Then suddenly it is gone.

Chapter 14

A peal of church bells resonating across the marsh gently reminded the boy that is was Sunday morning. He'd awoken to the sound of these enchanting chimes with a sense of pride and of a new belonging for he'd survived the night. And although he had to admit to himself that he hadn't slept very well, mainly due to the midge's and gnats which had driven him half mad with torment, he was still here, contrary to expectation, safe and sound in body and soul. Any doubts he'd harboured regarding the prudence of his daring enterprise had simply melted into nonexistence. He'd conquered his fear of the desolation of night and finally felt at peace with himself, free of all fear and sorrow.

The birds were busy chattering amongst themselves and the bright blue sky was void of any cloud. As he'd suspected it seemed as though it was going to be another very hot day. A thick, moist layer of muggy air had already descended upon the marsh and he began to feel sticky and uncomfortable. He felt thirsty and readily scolded himself for squandering his orange squash during the night. He stared down at his empty lemonade bottle and at the pool in which there must have been thousands of litres of water.

His throat was so dry he had a crazy notion to dive into it and drink every last drop. He could have boiled some of the pond water last night, he supposed and waited for it to have cooled. But he hadn't had anything to boil it in. He'd also exhausted his food supply but now that was only a minor hiccup compared to his water shortage. He never envisaged such a serious setback but he knew that in order to maintain his sustainability the problem needed addressing urgently. His priority today was to go in search of some fresh, clean water. Where to begin though? He knew that there was a public fountain up in Milton High Street near the old Court Hall but if he dared to go there he was bound to be noticed. No, he sighed, the risk was too great. He would just have to try his luck elsewhere.

As a matter of interest, the boy was fond of this adorable old building and had become quite familiar with its history. It has stood at the very heart of the village since around the mid 15th century during the reign of Henry VI. Indeed, like the quaint medieval church, he considered it the essence of Milton Regis which, incidentally is now a popular museum housing a collection of antiquated items of local historical and archaeological interest. Ever since Saxon times however, up until perhaps around the turn of the century, this important monument had always served as a court house. It was used by the Lord of the Manor of Milton whose prestigious position it was to maintain law and order throughout the town and district, occasionally enforcing court orders for the placement of disorderly Miltonians such as pickpockets, footpads and unruly, promiscuous whores into the stocks located just outside in the courtyard, for misdemeanours such as drunkenness or breach of the peace.

The curator had let slip that he believed a few of these

residing magistrates may have also been responsible for condemning one or two undesirable characters to their untimely deaths. Possibly sentenced to be hanged by their necks till they be dead at Maidstone or Eastchurch gaols. The boy had been horrified to learn that their corpses were encaged in iron gibbets and hung from gallows situated around the marshes and forsaken to rot, swinging to and fro in the bitter winter wind as a stark warning to cutthroat pirates and smugglers, murderous thieves and any other would-be outlaws.

Chapter 15

The sun burned intensely through a hazy, sultry atmosphere. Visibility was poor. The breeze had died away to a feathery whisper and the tide had receded to a harmless stream trickling its way back to the sea. Several swifts and swallows were showing off their aerobatical skills in a magnificent flying display and down at the ebb of the outgoing tide a dozen or so egrets were wading silently through the mud.

The boy had walked the entire length of the creek's coastal path from its mouth westside where it joins the Swale at Kemsley, all the way up to its head where the paper mill's concrete water tower stood, unsuccessful in his search for something to drink. His situation was becoming insidious and he began to debate whether he should ask the gypsy man if he could spare some of his drinking water. It might also be, he reasoned, an ideal excuse to get acquainted with him. Here, at the end of the sea wall, he got the feeling that he was being followed, the fine hairs on the nape of his neck felt prickly and his heart again began to drum with fear. He spun round sharply to investigate. But there was nobody there.

Before returning to the marsh, he took refuge for a while in the shade under the light railway viaduct. This unique construction, twenty feet high in places, belonged to Bowaters papermill. To the boy it rather resembled a giant concrete centipede, winding its way through the town on the back of which puffed steam locomotives hauling heavy goods and workmen along the narrow gauge line between the two paper-making mills sited at Sittingbourne and Kemsley.

Soon he began worrying again about the likelihood of being noticed by either the wise ones or any of his fellow parishioners, for here he was far too exposed. Without warning he was forced to duck down out of sight after noticing across the way someone who he needed to avoid at all costs. The person in question was Mrs Bertha Musgrave, a grey-haired, sour-faced woman. Fat with enormous wobbly arms who possessed the black eyes of a vulture, ravenous for any hint of a scandal. She was returning home from the town carrying bags full with shopping. She was also a blatant snitch. Deciding to leave sooner rather than later, he stripped to his waist and promptly headed back to the relative safety of the sea wall.

Later he heard the sounds of laughter coming from across the creek. When he looked over he noticed a small crowd of drinkers whom had gathered outside the Brickmaker's Arms. The public house stood facing the creek between the old cement mill and the brickworks. Naturally its patrons consisted mainly of mill workers and brickmakers. The men from mill were permanently plastered in grey cement dust, each looking like a different version of Jacob Marley's ghost. The brickmakers, especially the sorters whom handled the rough bricks day in day out, were reputed to have no fingerprints. Listening to their merriment and watching them supping their ale, he felt thirstier than ever.

A little farther along he saw a man in a blue boiler suit working alone on the bridge of the old paddle steamer. The boy noticed that he had a thermos flask which he guessed was probably full with hot tea. If the tide had been in, he knew he'd have no qualms about swimming across and asking to borrow some, such was his raging thirst.

Rather than admit defeat, he obstinately stuck to his plan and made for the potdigger's home over in the washbacks. Like earlier, he had a vague feeling that somebody or something was stalking him. Again, his heart rate increased and so did his pace. But out on the open marshes, again exposed to the merciless heat of the sun, he soon began to feel unwell. He was now sweating profusely and becoming weaker by the minute. An unnatural silence panned out across the hinterland as though some inexplicable phenomenon had sucked the day empty of time, cocooning everything that existed in a vacuum of space. He thought it the queerest feeling, as if the earth had stopped ticking like a broken clock. Feeling dizzy and nauseous he became unsteady on his feet. The stifling air began to strangle the life out of him and the unforgiving world about him began to spin. Now he felt certain that something catastrophic was about to occur. The lids of his eyes felt like heavy weights and he couldn't manage another step. Both his legs began to wobble before he finally collapsed to the ground.

Struggling to remain conscious his vision seriously began to blur and therefore he was only half aware of the dark figure fast approaching him. He believed it to be a man who was carrying something. A pole maybe…or an axe. This was the end, he thought. He was doomed and could offer up no resistance or opinion of voice when the stranger suddenly grabbed hold of him under his arms, scooping him up from the ground and slinging him over his broad shoulders like the dead carcass of an animal shot for trophy. Hanging helplessly he was now resigned to his fate. He could barely focus the skin on the back of the man's hands which seemed scaly, like that of a reptile's and he smelled of ashes and damp earth. Dehydrated, exhausted and totally disorientated, the boy tried to speak but the only sound his mouth could form was incoherent gobbledygook.

Chapter 16

The boy was so tired he felt he could have slept for a month. He hadn't even the strength to raise his eyelids but welcomed both the darkness and the silence. He was tucked up in between the cool sheets in his own sweet bed, of that he was convinced. How he'd got here and whom had fetched him remained arcane. But none of this abstruseness was troubling him. He didn't care. He felt safe and sound and that was all that mattered right now. He just wanted to sleep… and sleep…

And then suddenly he sees the baldheaded man. The one with the kind, scarlet face standing behind the steaming tea urn on the serving counter. The boy's lips are arid, cracked and peeling. His throat feels as dry as sandpaper. The man opens a bottle of ice-cold fizzy cola and hands it to him.

'But I haven't any money to pay for it,' explains the boy, earnestly. The man smiles and gives him the drink free of charge.

He thanks the café proprietor and then sits down at one of the Formica tables. Gratefully, he quivers with delight sipping the cool, refreshing cola up through a red and white striped paper straw. Thousands of bubbles explode on his tongue and it tastes of America. He imagines Cowboys and Indians, drive-in movies and hot dogs, popcorn and Malborough cigarettes, elongated convertibles with real cow horns on the bonnets, Las Vegas and tictactoe fruit machines and Elvis Presley.

He believes he's in the Hasty Tasty café, situated in Milton High Street next door to the undertakers and he very much hopes that Christopher Crispin is safely hidden away indoors out of the way of prying eyes where he cannot unwittingly give him away. The Beatles latest hit record 'Hey Jude' is playing on the Wurlitzer Jukebox.

An old tramp that frequents the village is seated on the opposite table. Rodger the dodger reminds him of a scarecrow with his thick, oily, bedraggled mop of hair and long Father Christmas beard. The tramp is wearing a great heavy coat which hangs from his ears to his ankles and on his feet, surprisingly, are a pair of highly polished brown English gentlemen's brogues which the boy assumes he's probably cadged off of some poor unsuspecting widow. The vagrant sleeps wherever he can. In shop doorways or dark alleyways or under the stars in pleasant weather. Sometimes, he'd even fallen unconscious whilst leaning up against the old Court Hall in a drunken stupor. Scratching at his flea bites, he coughs and splutters and curses his ailments for all to hear with particular reference to his poor old bunions.

The café owner, stretched to the limit of his patience, reprimands the old man and issues him a final verbal warning and this time he promises, he really means it!

Rodger the dodger bows his head, groans a little quieter, slurps up his tea which he has poured into a saucer and then munches noisily on his cold buttered toast.

A middle-aged woman with a blue rinse hairdo plays the one-armed bandit. She's dressed smartly in a black and white dogtooth coat and a pair of white patent stilettos. She is also wearing a pair of light blue plastic framed spectacles with the side parts curled up like an Edwardian man's moustaches. Protruding from the centre of the gaming machine is a sculptured brass head of a Native American Indian chief. Portraying a staunch expression, he fiercely guards the glittering prize on display beyond a small glass panel below. Five pounds worth of brand new shillings represents the jackpot to tempt the punter into parting with her own hard earnt shillings.

The boy remains watchful as the lady yanks down the handle which sets the three reels of chance spinning. The first reel clunks to a halt and the jackpot bars are shown. The second reel follows suit and again the jackpot bars have dropped into position. The blue rinse woman shrieks with excitement for she is on the verge of landing the Red Indian's sparkling reward.

The boy looks on with as much anticipation. Alas, all of the gambling woman's expectations are abruptly and most misfortunately shattered when the third and final set of jackpot bars slide tantalizingly by and is replaced by a worthless cherry displayed in a final klunkclick!

'Oh fiddlesticks!' cries the disappointed woman, 'fiddlesticks and damnation!' she adds, as she makes her hurried and premature exit.

He continues to observe the woman in disarray through the café's large bay windows as she crosses the road and enters Barclay's Bank, to replenish her lost shillings no doubt.

He finishes his drink and gets up to bid the kind proprietor farewell. After he closes the café door behind him, he remembers that he has forgotten his straw hat. But curiously, when he tries to regain entry, he discovers the door now to be locked. Even more bizarre, when peering back through the glass panel in the door, he can plainly see that the café is in darkness and there is nobody there. He also notices the sign hanging down on the inside that says CLOSED.

He proceeds along the high street somewhat puzzled before he then accidently bumps into shell-shocked Lonny. The old man is holding a grimy handkerchief against his jaw-locked open mouth which continuously dribbles saliva. Lon's gaze is fixed permanently towards the open sky in search of German doodlebugs. From his austere bedsit room above the chip shop he roams to and fro the recreation ground where a Second World War siren stands before some disused, boarded up air raid shelters, constantly in a state of nervous readiness to escape Hitler's bombs. The boy listens caringly to the old man's superfluous apocalyptic warnings that nobody else nowadays ever pays any attention to. He feels sorry for the poor, wretched man and his suffering and so attempts to greet him a hearty good day but suddenly the forgotten hero is nowhere to be seen.

As the boy passes under the town's clock it strikes twelve o'clock noon. Midday, but oddly enough there isn't another pedestrian present and neither is there any traffic. All the shops are open and their billboards are on the pavements advertising their business. But where are the customers? On closer inspection he also notices that there isn't anyone serving at the cash registers either. A thief could have himself an away day, stealing anything his heart so desired and nobody would have been any the wiser. The situation seems preposterous to the boy.

Where is everybody? He asks himself, a little worryingly for the high street possesses the forlorn air of a ghost town. Even on a Sunday there was usually someone around to talk to. But there is nobody at all. Not even a stray dog or a prowling cat. And where have all the birds gone?

Now he yearns only for the sanctuary of the boy's dormitory. He must make haste and get back to Greenporch and so without any further hesitation he sprints off home as fast as he can. Shooting down Cross Lane by the old Court Hall, into Brewery Road past the Butts School and down on to the marsh road. He never lets up his furious pace until he reaches the garden gate of his faithful orphanage.

Suddenly his heart leaps up into his throat. Impeding the way is the man they call Blackberry Bill. He seems awfully angry and there are fresh blood stains around his mouth. He is yielding a sharp looking dagger which he menacingly sways to and fro as he edges towards the terrified boy.

The boy shuts his eyes in disgust for he feels his own slaughter is imminent. Without warning the ground beneath his feet begins to shake and crumble. Suddenly it implodes and the next thing he is aware of is lying face down on a heap of rubble, coughing acutely in a cloud of brown dust. After the powdery dirt settles, he begins to understand that he has by chance discovered the secret passageway, albeit by some very timely and miraculous intervention.

Surprised by the fact that he has suffered no ill effect through this extraordinary occurrence he interprets this strange situation as something divine. He peers down the shaft of the tunnel that is illuminated by burning candles fixed intermediately all along the route. Excited by the challenge it invites, he quickly brushes himself down and sets forth.

With his scary black shadow on the wall creeping behind in his wake, threatening and poised to pounce at the moment he should dare to drop his guard, he proceeds hesitantly along the passageway where he soon begins to notice pieces of human bone poking out of the earth ceiling. Whilst studying them above his head, he loses his balance and clumsily trips up over something lying on the ground. Here he is startled by the discovery of a complete human skeleton at rest before his feet. He wonders if it had originally come from the graveyard above having fallen through. Or had something more sinister occurred here?

He begins to worry and get scared but then remembers something which old Mr Stickles, the caretaker, had once told him.

'Never be afraid of the dead young laddie...the dead ain't going to hurt you because they're dead...but the living can!'

He scans the tunnel with dilated pupils for any clue of the maniac Blackberry Bill and listens scrupulously...Nothing but eerie silence. When the end of the passageway is in sight, he notices how it broadens and the abundance of brightly burning candles. Scores of tiny flames all of a flutter, dancing wildly as if suddenly excited by his presence. He compares the scene to a picture he'd once seen in a school book of Aladin's cave, except this place exhibited no gold and silver coins or jewellery and precious gems. He sighs slightly disgruntled, for the treasure that confronts him is merely a collection of worthless clay jugs and glass bottles stacked from the floor to the ceiling and crammed into every nook and cranny.

Between these hundreds and thousands of pots and bottles there is a narrow gap just wide enough for him to squeeze through. Beyond it he sees a flight of stone steps which lead upwards into the darkness. With some trepidation, he slowly climbs the stairs until he reaches the top. Here it is pitch dark so he is forced to feel his way blindly along the wall until he is eventually hindered by a further wall which inhibits his progress altogether. Fretfully, he gropes about the stonework either side of him and directly in front of him but finds that he cannot proceed any farther. He appears to be trapped and begins to panic. A compulsion to press his full weight hard against the obstruction pays dividend. To his relief, he discovers that he has managed to push the wall or door or whatever it is open slightly outward. Through a small crack daylight floods in and encourages the boy to push harder still until he eventually opens it completely. At last he is free and out in the familiar surroundings of Milton Churchyard.

He is thrilled to have finally discovered the entrance of the mythical secret tunnel which so happened to be the large stone mausoleum next to his own parents' grave.

Cutting his elation short however, was the unwelcome sight of Blackberry Bill sitting on the tombstone above the entrance. He'd been waiting there to intercept his prey and this time he is armed with an axe. The boy prays for the ground beneath his feet to collapse a further time as the mad man leaps down onto the grave before him, effectively blocking him in between the tomb and the churchyard wall. Now he was trapped. The axe man grins through his crooked mouth as his raises the weapon above his head. The boy, sensing the end is nigh, screws up his eyes tight and screams out as loud as his young lungs will bellow.

Chapter 17

The boy awoke in a cold sweat, breathing frantically with his thoughts, which were clouded in turmoil. Earlier he would have sworn that he was in the boy's dormitory back at Greenporch. Now evidently he was sat bolt upright in someone else's bed and he had an awful inkling it was Blackberry Bill's.

Anxiously he tried to recall what had happened. He remembered fainting, no doubt due to a serious case of sunstroke. He'd also a vague recollection of the stranger seizing hold of him down on the sea wall. But then after that there was nothing. Exasperated, he tried to rack his brains but here his mind had gone completely blank.

Conscious of his facial skin, which was puffy and had peeled quite noticeably, he was also aware that his lips were chafed and a little swollen. However, apart from these relatively minor complaints, which weren't too painful, he was feeling pretty much all right. So now he finally dropped his shoulders and tried to relax a little. Whoever this stranger was, he deduced, he clearly bore him no malice. He'd obviously taken good care of him and was hardly then the sort of person who would hurt him or God forbid even eat him.

This was indeed the potdigger's home. Its contents had persuaded him of that for it was also cluttered with the same stuff identical to the bottles and pots he'd seen stacked up outside. Except these particular examples were sparkling clean and they'd been placed carefully on the ledges and shelves as prized ornaments.

Positioned in what seemed to be pride of place however, above the artificial fireplace, was a large silver framed black and white photograph. The image portrayed a proud faced, middle-aged gypsy woman wearing large hooped gold earrings and a plain dark scarf. Stood beside her was a young man clad in a plain white shirt, striped waistcoat and dark breeches. Both were smiling, mildly embarrassed and posing for the camera before a bowtop vardo not unlike the one he was in, in what seemed to be a cherry orchard.

He scoured the walls and shelves but there didn't seem to be anymore photographs on display. He made a mental inventory of everything around him. On a wooden side cabinet there was neatly laid an ornate dinner service and hanging from the ceiling on bits of string were some copper pots and pans. There was an unusual looking black iron stove with a stainless steel kettle placed upon it. To the side of the cooker was a wooden tub full to the brim with potatoes and a mixture of fresh vegetables. Stacked up on top of a cupboard unit were some jars containing cereal, biscuits, sugar and tea. There was also a plentiful supply of tinned food such as rice, baked beans and garden peas.

He decided to get up out of the bed and steal a glance at the outside world. With exception of his underpants, he then realised, somewhat mortified, that he was naked but instantly noticed his clothes neatly folded and piled up on a chair next to his rucksack. The upper half of the vardo's stable type door had been left wide open and clamped in position by the hook. This was proof then that he hadn't been taken prisoner, he thought.

Outside everything was very much as before, completely peppered with hundreds of jars and bottles but with one important difference, Blackberry Bill was nowhere to be seen. Now was his chance to escape.

As he hurried to get dressed he couldn't help noticing the scrap book lying on the table. The album had been carelessly left open at a page where at some point in bygone years the man had adhered a couple of newspaper columns. They'd yellowed with age but were still perfectly readable. He now dressed more slowly, purposely stalling for time. His curiosity was burning. Perhaps he should take a peek. Maybe this Blackberry Bill had intended for him to see it all along.

He wondered where the potdigger had gone. Had he been that worried about him to go and telephone the doctors? He sincerely hoped not and besides it would be a waste of both the man's time and energy for he felt perfectly well now. Here he paused and wondered why he wasn't feeling thirsty anymore. Or hungry come to that. And why had Blackberry Bill gone to so much trouble to help him? he pondered, slowly beginning to believe him wholly innocuous rather than this dangerous maniac the travellers had made him out to be. His unfavourable reputation seemed grossly unjust.

Perhaps they'd all been too quick to judge this man on hearsay alone, he thought. He'd awoken in his home feeling safe and well. It was very clean and comfortable too. Why should he now be frightened of such a person? And so what if he has this crazy idea about digging up the entire marshes. Was that such a terrible thing?

Now content to sit down at the small table and browse the album, he noticed, enthralled by the discovery as he flicked through, that all the other pages were blank. Only two paper cuttings had been posted into the book which had originally been published in February and March, 1958, a little over a decade ago, by the local gazette. The reports read as follows;

First tabloid cutting: '*BABY BOY RESCUED BY UNKNOWN HERO*' were the paper's front page headlines. '*Emergency services were rushed to the scene of a serious blaze on Friday evening last at approximately 8.30pm at Milton Creek wharf. It is thought that the fire, which had completely destroyed at least six vessels on the creek, had originated from 'The Marianne' sailing barge boat.*

Two additional fire engines and their crews were summoned from surrounding boroughs to assist. Together they had fought for over three hours to bring the blaze under control.

Sadly the owners of 'The Marianne', Mr Thomas Langley 48 and his wife Isobella Langley 41, had both suffered first degree burns and consequently later died as a result of their injuries. However, their infant son Thomas Langley junior had been miraculously saved by a young unemployed drifter who happened to be loitering in the vicinity and whom it is believed was the first person at the scene and participant of the rescue attempt. As a consequence of his gallant efforts, he'd also been severely burnt and was rushed to East Grinstead hospital for emergency medical treatment.

With exception of the local police the vagabond has refused to be interviewed, especially by the media and has chosen to remain anonymous. However, in admiration and respect for a truly brave young man, and on behalf of all our readers and the staff here at The Gazette, we salute you sir and wish you a very speedy recovery.

Three cheers then for our unknown hero. Hip, hip, hooray! Hip, hip, hooray! Hip, hip, hooray!'

The follow up report that had appeared in the stop press some weeks later read as follows;

'The inquest's findings recorded that there had been no evidence of foul play forthcoming in this case and subsequently verdicts of accidental deaths were accepted and duly registered by the coroner resident.

It was further suggested by a member of the brigade's forensic investigation department that an upset oil lit lantern was the probable cause of this fatal fire. Its cargo aside, the vessel had not been covered for insurance purposes.'

Chapter 18

As the boy stepped outside the caravan, he wavered slightly before slumping down onto the seat beside an upturned tub that doubled as an outside table. Now in receipt of this knowledge which had knocked him for six he could hardly breathe. It seemed to him that this man Blackberry Bill, or whoever he really is, had actually saved his life. Why else should he have kept the cuttings? He asked himself, convinced that this was the case. And those blemishes all over his body were not blackberry stains and neither were they bloodstains. They were burns. But what had compelled this stranger to risk his own life to save that of a baby boy who'd meant nothing to him? He was undeniably in this man's debt. He must wait for him to return, he reasoned, if only to thank him. He sat flabbergasted staring out at nothing in particular, his mind bombarded with hypothetical questions and whirling with thoughts of remorse.

He ruminated. And to think that once upon a time he'd considered this man a monster. A stranger deemed dark and sinister, someone to be feared and hated. But the reality is that the poor wretch has continuously suffered one way or another ever since that dreadful night of the fire when he'd so selflessly put his own life in jeopardy. The boy was very much regretting his own misconceptions and was at a loss as to why this extraordinary man should have tolerated his miserable existence here for so long, having been constantly misunderstood by the villagers and subjected to their superstitious nonsense and mindless ridicule.

For another hour or so he sat and twiddled his thumbs and wondered about the implications of what he'd discovered. How does one thank somebody for saving their life? Especially when that person has suffered so much as a result of their brave deeds. But there was still no trace of the man and it was only then that something else suddenly dawned on him. Judging by the position of the sun he realised that today cannot possibly be Sunday. This meant of course that he'd therefore spent the whole night lying in the gypsy's caravan and now it was in actual fact Monday morning. The weather had changed as well. Today the sky was partly cloudy and the high temperature of yesterday had plummeted somewhat.

Although the boy was growing a little impatient, he remained determined to meet this man. To distract himself, he began to examine more closely the artifacts spread around him. Among the diverse range of wares were some pot lids which had been separated from their bases. They came in a variety of shapes and sizes and were amassed into different categories according to what each pot had originally contained. Some of the lids portrayed advertisements printed underneath a glazed finished surface describing various products such as cherry toothpastes from Boots the Chemists or anchovy paste from J. Sainsbury's. Others said that they were cold creams or healing ointments and there was one in particular called Bear's grease, he couldn't imagine what peculiar substance that might be.

A few of these lids had pictures on them too. Beautiful coloured landscapes like those of the old masters which he'd seen hanging in the national gallery. One of the coloured lids, which he rather liked, pictated a scene of some Victorian Kentish fishermen hauling in their catch with their fishing nets at Pegwell Bay.

All the while he'd been waiting for the man to return home something else had been troubling him. He'd already accepted that the pot digging man must have been the same young unemployed drifter whom had rescued him as a baby and for that he owed him his life and his deepest gratitude. All the same the question still remained. If indeed his rescuer was also the same person who was regularly leaving the flowers on the grave then what was the connection between this man and his mother and father?

Bursting to find out the truth, he couldn't wait a moment longer and so set off in search of him towards the open marshes. Fortunately, no sooner after exiting the washback, he'd beheld him straight away. As always the man was digging for pots and had (all the time the boy had been waiting) been no more than fifty metres away. In his hands he was clutching, not a pole or an axe or a dagger or any other dangerous weapon but a plain old garden digging fork. Confirming the boy's recent change of heart and opinion of him and rather than this angry and unpredictable villain that he'd always imagined him to be, the man's nature now appeared to be more congenial and placid. The boy proceeded towards him feeling comfortable and happy to do so.

The man then halted in his toil after noticing the boy approaching, apprehensively zigzagging his way through the scores of little potholes like bomb craters and disturbing a dissimulation of birds en-route taking flight all around him.

As he got nearer he noted that the gypsy seemed just as curious of him. Slowly and without uttering a sound they studied each other, weighing up one another like two gunfighters in a spaghetti western.

At last he was now face to face with the man he'd so desperately wanted to talk to. But now both man and boy were reluctant to speak, each careful with their emotions, not wanting to display any weakness of character.

The boy, offering to break the ice, said, 'I wish to introduce myself, my name…'

However, before he'd had the chance to finish his sentence the man interrupted him. 'I know who you are, boy!' he claimed, uttering his words slowly in a deep, husky voice.

The boy was intrigued. The man's eyes, staring down at him, seem to hide some dark secret.

'You're young Tommy Langley from that kid's home yonder,' he added, pointing out in the general direction of Greenporch.

The man's statement had completely flummoxed the boy for he hadn't the remotest idea of how the stranger would have possibly known him by sight only. Despite this, he remained sceptical about the cook's belief that certain individuals among the gypsy clans possessed the power to predict the future. 'But how do you know who I am?' he retorted.

The man stared at him as if he were an imbecile. 'Your bag boy…. It says so in your bag!'

'Oh yes,' agreed the boy feeling slightly foolish, remembering that his rucksack did indeed contain his name and address written on a label sewn into the lining. He'd forgotten all about that.

'I know a bit about words,' explained the man, as he made the sign of the cross. 'My mother, God bless'er, learned me some when I was only a chavvie myself…You think I can't read'em then?'

'No, I didn't think that sir,' replied the boy, blushing and contrite.

'Sir now, is it?' returned the man in jest. 'You thought I was going to eat you it was the night before, taken over with it, you was.'

'I don't quite follow,' said the boy, abashed and somewhat bemused.

'Hollering out in your kip…Don't eat me, please don't eat me Bill,' mimicked the man, enjoying himself at the boy's expense. 'God knows who this Bill is.'

Embarrassed, the boy lowered his head and began to clam up. Sensing this, the man owned up. 'I'm only jeeing you up boy…Say what you was going to say.'

The boy chose to remain uncommunicative for a while and so the gypsy shrugged his shoulders and resumed his pot digging. But the boy had been thinking about the newspaper articles and a short time later asked, 'It was you wasn't it?'

'Of course it was me!' retorted the man, believing that the boy was referring to his help only yesterday. 'It was me who helped you…who'd you think it was then?'

The boy nearly said that he'd always assumed that it was one of his parents whom had rescued him but the man continued.

'Nobody ever comes over here anymore…You was lucky I saw you when I did because you was proper wafti boy. I didn't think you looked very well, that's why I shadowed you half-way across the marshes and brought you back here. You'd copped a big dose of that sun I reckon. But too much of old Phoebe can make you sick and dizzy and she'd took hold good and hard all night, and all the while you was talking jibberish.'

The man had clearly got hold of the wrong end of the stick but the boy said nothing and just listened.

'But I got that water down you boy,' the man revealed, looking pleased with himself, 'plenty of cups full too along a bowl of hot simmin.'

The boy's facial expression contorted into one of disarray trying to understand the man's unintelligible dialect.

The man reiterates, 'Soup, boy, a bowl of soup!'

The gypsy had given the boy shade from the burning sun, sustained him on soup and bread and most importantly rehydrated him with clean water. His kind deeds had dragged him back from the brink of death. He'd saved his life as an infant and now as a boy. But what could he do for the man in return? he wondered. How could he ever repay the compassion this man has shown him?

'I'm so very grateful to you sir.'

'Well don't be!' returned the man, making light of the whole episode. 'And don't keep calling me sir, my name is Tom, same as yooze.'

This was rather a surprise for he'd expected him to say Bill, quickly deciding that it was probably wiser not to question this. All the same he was pleased to have at least something, if only something as trivial as Christian names, in common with this odd but benign individual and he felt something akin to friendship shroud his little heart.

'Are you hungry?' asked the man, genially.

Having now regained his appetite the boy smiled and nodded convivially.

'Come on then boy,' said the man, climbing back out of the trench he'd dug. 'Help us carry these sacks of pots back home and we'll have some nosh and a good old natter too, what d'you say?'

Chapter 19

Meanwhile, back at Greenporch, Mr Stickles had felt it necessary to go and knock on the office door.

'Come in,' cried Mrs Saffron. She was sitting at her desk sorting through the mail. 'Good morning Wally,' she said cheerfully. 'It's not often we're graced with your presence,' she added in playful jest. 'What's the problem?'

Walter Stickles removed his cloth cap and held it respectfully at his midriff. In his gruff voice he spoke each of his words slowly and carefully.

'The bird mam, don't seem right at all.' The gardener come caretaker frequently fed the jackdaw titbits and nattered to it on a daily basis. But he'd noticed yesterday that the bird wasn't quite itself and this morning it'd seemed even worse. He'd grown quite attached to the boy's pet and he was worried.

'Jack! What's the matter with him then?'

'Don't rightly know mam, but I reckon he's sorely depressed. Possibly missing the boy.'

'Well I'm afraid young Tommy's staying over at his friend's house at the moment. If he's not back by tomorrow, Wally, I'll give Mr Crispin a call.'

More or less satisfied with her decision, Mr Stickles then said, 'Right'o mam, I'll get back to my tomatoes then.'
'Thank you for letting me know, Wally.'

Chapter 20

Like long-lost friends they walked back over to the washback, occasionally detouring left and right to avoid falling down into any of the old excavations. The boy was curious to know why the man had dug so many holes.

'For the pots and bottles boy,' explained the man.

'Yes, but why have you collected so many?'

'Klexem... I don't klexem, I sells'em boy!' declared the man. 'That's how I makes me living, ain't it...See, when I've got a half decent load of cushti gear I run it down on the train to a gadgie I know in Canterbury...I've known him, old Henry for years and years. He's got a gaff down there called *Ye old bottle shoppe*...Heard of it, boy?'

The boy shook his head.

'Yeah, well Henry, he buys all my stuff and pays me a half tidy sum for it too... And then he works'em into the foreign gadgies... Yanks and Canadians mostly.'

The boy was astonished to learn that good folk had actually paid this man real cash for what was basically a load of old rubbish.

A crafty smirk formed across the man's disfigured face, 'It's a right cushti living I've made for myself out here on these boodiful marshes and I'm sure my father, God bless'im.' At this point he stopped briefly to lower the sack clenched in his right hand to make another sign of the cross. 'I'm sure he would've been proud of me.' The boy secretly agreed with him for he was proud of him as well.

But just as they were about to set off again the man suddenly grabbed hold of the boy's shoulder and pulled him aside, narrowly avoiding a nest of vipers lying camouflaged in between tufts of grass. Having always loathed snakes, the boy gasped in abhorrence and was about to stamp on one of the baby adders wriggling away to safety but was held firm by the man.

'Leave it alone boy!' he demanded. 'A serpent is still one of the Lord's critters and it deserves to live like yooze and me. To harm it would be worse than the curse of a cross-eyed man, you can trust my word on that one.'

Realising the danger, the boy began to appreciate the fact that although the marshes were teeming with wildlife not all of it was harmless. They continued on once more.

'I've got hundreds and thousands in the Hastings and Thanet Building Society,' the man boasted before suddenly stopping dead again. Considering that maybe he'd divulged too much, he turned and bent down level with the boy's head so as to look him straight in the eye.

'Here, don't you go telling anyone about all of this, will you boy…Because I'd have'em down here, if they should get the slightest whisper, scratching about just like them scabby rats over on the dump if you so dared to blab.'

'I won't tell anyone,' promised the boy. 'Cross my heart and hope to die.'

The man studied his new friend suspiciously. 'Will you take an oath on it?'

'I swear not to tell a soul sir, honest I won't.'

The man scratched the stubble on his chin with his grubby fingers and chewed on the boy's words for a moment or two. After making up his mind, he dropped the sack of pots, spat into the palm of his hand and offered it to the boy as a token of solidarity. Relieved with having gained the man's trust, the boy repeated the spitting ritual and wholeheartedly shook the gypsy's hand in friendship.

'Good then!' said the man, patting the boy's back and seemingly satisfied with his young companion's promise. 'Now how about that grub, I could murder a cup of rosie. Let's jel off out of here.'

Shortly before entering the washback the gypsy halted yet again and gently placed his laden sack to the ground. Holding his right index finger up to his puckered lips, he gestured for quietness. 'Shoosh now boy!' he demanded, whilst pointing over at a nearby grassy bank clothed in thick gorse.

The boy put down his own sack of bottles and itched with curiosity as the man slowly led him by the hand over towards the brambles.

'Look there!' whispered the gypsy, creeping up closer.

The boy's eyes opened wide with joy and amazement when he saw the fox curled up asleep outside of its den. The vixen's beautiful russet coat shone with health but she was lying there dead to the world completely unaware of her approving audience.

Studying the animal further, the boy's heart skipped a beat. 'It isn't dead is it, Tom?'

'Nar, of course she ain't, don't talk divvy,' explained the gypsy. 'Dik at her belly, she's breathing…Most likely been hunting rabbits half the night, hungry cubs maybe.'

Overhead storm clouds were gathering, darkening the sky and the wind was beginning to gain momentum and by the time they'd got back to the caravan it had started to rain hard. The boy was famished but once they were inside and in the dry the gypsy was as good as his word. He fried eggs and bacon and served them up on doorstep slices of toast which they washed down with mugs of hot sweet tea. The boy noticed that the album had been deliberately tucked away somewhere. He also hadn't yet plucked up the courage to ask about the flowers on the grave, the question repeatedly refusing to leave the tip of his tongue. He flumped back in the chair with his belly about to pop. 'Thank you Tom, that was truly scrumptious.'

'You're welcome, boy.'

Staring up at the happy people in the framed photograph above the fireplace, the boy wondered whom they might be. Noticing his curiosity the man then also gazed up at it and smiled, reminiscing over happier times. 'It's me and my mother, love her heart.' The young man and the woman were like two peas in a pod. Both were beautiful and vibrant with life. 'That was taken years back, picking gurlos for a farmer we knew in Teynham, not far from here… Cushti old days them.'

The boy was somewhat puzzled because his friend didn't look anything like the image of the young good looking man in the picture but shrugged it off as the truth. He looked out of the tiny window at all of the pottery scattered about. 'How did you discover that the pots were worth money?' he asked. He still couldn't quite comprehend their status as items of value.

The man placed the dirty plates and cutlery into his washing up bowl before filling his pipe with fresh tobacco and making himself comfortable on the bed. 'I stumbled on'em quite by accident really… when I first came here,' he began. He lit his pipe and grinned guilefully. 'But as soon as I'd clapped my yoks on'em I knew what they were and I knew then an all that they were worth a bob or two.' Outside it was thundering and lightning and pelting down with rain so he was forced to pause a while until the sound of the raindrops drumming on the roof had lessened.

'Because I'd seen'em before you see, the pots. Many times, in the windows of the antique shops on my travels with my poor dear mother.' Again he respects his mother by creating the sign of the cross.

'Because they sell this stuff all over Kent and Sussex you know… And up in London an all I dare say… One of them shop gadgies told me he'd got a posh mush from the television people. BBC, ain't it?'

The boy nodded in agreement, watching the raindrops trickle down the outside of the window pane. The heavy downpour had ceased but it was still quite blustery.

'Anyway, this BBC bloke buys off him regular like. They use'em as props or somemink for their old-fashioned telly programmes… It's the Americans though that likes'em the best for history and that.' The man paused again and then said, 'When I've rested a while boy, I want to show you somemink.' He put down his pipe, closed his eyes and spoke no more.

Chapter 21

After the man had awoken from his nap, he put the kettle on the stove and called out to his young friend. 'Do you want a cup of tea, boy?'

The rain had finally cleared up and the sun had come out again. The boy had been amusing himself just outside the caravan, stacking up the various pots and bottles and rearranging them into different shapes. 'Umm, yes please... Look Tom, I've made a potcastle.'

The gypsy slowly shook his sleepy head. He wasn't much impressed and tutted his rare annoyance. 'See that lid you've got on top there.' He was referring to a potlid which had a picture of Queen Victoria's head on it. 'That's worth a couple of nicker!'

Sensing something was wrong, the boy asked, 'What was it that you wanted to show me then?'

The man rubbed his tired eyes and yawned himself more alert before scratching his ribs with both hands. 'There's a decent spot I know where I sometimes go to do a bit of fishing...Just wondered if maybe you'd like to come along.'

The boy was pleased and nodded his accord. He had an idea that they were headed back to the secret island in the cornfield. 'What are we going to catch them with?' he asked, excitedly.

'I've got some poles round here somewhere,' replied the gypsy, searching amongst his chattels stored beside the vardo. 'And as for bait, well we can dig a few juicy ones up on the way.'

A short while later the gypsy led his young friend towards a long, narrow field which appeared to the boy as though it was completely draped in red velvet from one end to the other and then a little later like a gigantic abrasion on the green skin of the countryside. Smothered in a carpet of scarlet poppies, it gently sloped down to the mouth of the creek where the waters flowed out wide into the Swale. Just beyond was the jetty where the barges came in on the tide to unload their cargoes of coal destined for the paper mill's powerhouse. Swinging their fishing rods and bucket of earthworms, the gypsy and the boy gradually sauntered across the beautiful meadow with the wind in their sails and as happy as larks.

Soon they were both sat with their legs dangling over the side of the wooden pier which the gypsy had personally dubbed *Poppy Wharf*. The sea level was just right and it was the perfect spot from which to drop a line.

After they had carefully baited their hooks and cast their fishing lines, the gypsy filled his pipe with tobacco and lit it. 'I saw a couple of seals here once,' he claimed, puffing contentedly on his pipe and staring out at the calm waters. 'Just after the surge…must have got swept upstream I'd imagine.'

'What happened to them?' asked the boy, with interest.

'Dunno, never saw'em again. But I spose they'd got back safe to the sea.'

The boy, full of anticipation, was so excited by what he might hook and was pondering what it may of felt like to have actually done this with his father, had the circumstances been different. 'Did you ever go fishing with your dad?' he asked, wonderingly and clutching both the rod and reel with such undue force as though he was expecting to land something as substantial as say *Moby Dick.*

The gypsy hesitated, 'When I was a chavvie I never knew my real father, he replied, with the words sticking in his throat. 'Never even found out his name, not until just before my mother had snuffed it, God bless'er.' he added, crossing himself. 'But I think if you don't mind I'll tell you about him later.'

The boy paused, considering it probably best not to pursue the topic.

'Uncle Elijah took me fishing quite a lot though.' Revealed the gypsy. 'I'll say that for him, night fishing too.' After pausing briefly he then added, 'Umm, but then he did make me carry the tilley lamp and lug all that heavy gear about an all…It was him though who learned me to fish properly. And he showed me how to snare a rabbit. When I think back, they were the only two decent things he did do for me. And I'm not so sure if we weren't poaching most of the time either. Still, that was then and this is now.'

'Was Elijah your mother's brother?'

'Nar, he wasn't my proper uncle, not by blood any rate. That's just what my mother said I had to call him…Anyway, the less said about Eli, the better!'

Once again the boy dropped the subject and a little while later asked, 'What sort of fish can we catch around here then, Tom?'

'Ah, now let me think…We got dabs…And we got

flounders…And maybe, if we're proper fortuned, we got sea bass too.'

'What do you do with your catch after you've netted it?' asked the boy, wondering if perhaps he was expected to throw his fish back.

'Well I fry'em and eat'em of course!' returned the gypsy, beaming with delight. The taste of his most recent fish supper lingered on a recollection, wetting his appetite.

'Tom,' the boy hesitated. 'Can I come pot digging with you tomorrow?'

'Why d'you want to do that then?'

'Well I was hoping to find some really good pots, so I can sell them to that man in the Canterbury shop and get lots of money like you.'

Following a pause for some serious thought, the gypsy then asked, 'And what for you need wongur?'

The boy, not surprisingly, was stumped for an answer and so could only shrug his shoulders in ignorance.

Succeeding another short spell of consideration the gypsy then followed up with, 'But it ain't a mucha, boy.'

The boy frowned, 'Pardon?'

'I said it ain't much.'

'What isn't?'

'The spondulicks!'

The boy still didn't understand and screwed up his face accordingly.

'Well I know I've got a fair bit of it down in the old society but like I say it ain't much of a concern to me. You see, digging up the pots just sort of gives me somemink to do like. Otherwise I'd probably end up divvy I spose. But the wongur boy, it ain't really that important…Fair enough, I can buy my grub with it and a bit of clobber here and there and not forgetting my bacca too,' explained the gypsy, before his dark eyes began to scan the wide open sky. 'But it don't buy the sun and the moon up there, do it? And it don't buy the wind and the rain and all the boodiful flowers what grow round here. Or the fox I showed you, when she comes to see me from time to time and not least the birds what sing to me every morning…can't buy none of that, can it?'

The boy stared blankly at the man, seemingly still none the wiser.

'So don't yooze go concerning yourself too much about the greenbacks boy,' continued the gypsy, now much regretting mentioning his bank account in the first place. 'There's time enough for that when you've grown up.'

But the boy continued to stare at him bewilderingly.

The gypsy shook his head a little frustrated. 'Well, what I mean to say, what I'm trying to tell you boy, is that the best things in life will cost you nixes, so it ain't worth fretting over.'

The rain held off and it was a pleasant thing just to sit by the water's edge with not a care in the world and with their hearts filled to the brim with hope. Blending in with the natural serenity, with the warmth of the sun on their arms and their faces, they quietly and gently drifted off into themselves. For a long while they sat silent, basking in their own daydreams until a dinghy came sailing by. An old man in a dark coat with a long, grey beard was seated at the tiller. The gypsy was a tad concerned about the possible disruption to his fishing line but the boy was more interested in the vessel itself and was waving to the sailor. The old mariner in the little boat saw the boy and waved back.

The gypsy noticed the boy's interest and asked, 'Like the boats do you?'

The boy smiled wishfully. 'I dream about having my

own boat one day, Tom,' he replied, his gaze expanding far beyond the reed beds of the floodplain. 'I'd sail her out on the big blue sea to America. Then back to Africa. And then all the way to Australia as well.'

The gypsy grinned slyly. 'I know where there's one,' he claimed, hoping to please the boy.

The boy's ears pricked up and his eyes glowed jubilantly.

'Lying there just for the taking it is, up at the head of the creek. Granted, it's got a hole or two in it. But I reckon with a decent bit of wood from down oddzee's yard and a good lick of paint, we can get her fixed up all right. I can promise you that. I'll take you up to see it later, if you like.'

The boy was ecstatic and felt as though he might imminently burst into a million bubbles of pure happiness. Overjoyed by the gypsy's pledge and relaxing his grip on the fishing rod, he leant over and appreciatively cuddled the man with such warmth and emotion like he would have his own father. And in that tender, tearful moment he thought perhaps he should never return home again.

The boy's simple display of affection had deeply touched the gypsy's heart. 'Now there's an idea,' he proposed, pulling himself together. 'Maybe when we get her all shipshape and seaworthy, we can do some proper angling out there,' he said, pointing way beyond the Swale towards the North Sea. His rod then began to shudder and bow with tension. 'Hold up boy,' he chuckled. 'I think we've finally hooked one!'

Chapter 22

They'd spent the whole afternoon fishing from off the coal jetty. The boy had never felt this happy in his entire life. He and the gypsy were becoming better and better friends. Between the pair of them they had managed to catch a full hand of dabs which they'd gutted and cleaned and were now frying in the pan. Before they sat down to eat them, the boy asked, beseechingly, if he could stay for a further night.

'Please yourself young'n but you'll have to sling yourself under the vardo tonight because I need my bed. Never got much kip the night before on account of you being ill an all.'

The boy expressed some doubt, thinking that this meant perhaps he was going to have to sleep rough on the bare ground.

The man emitted a slight titter. 'Don't look so worried boy, you'll be snuggled up nicely in the old hammock…You never know, maybe the badgers will come and say hello.'

During the meal, the boy's focus was continually drawn to the black and white photograph hanging over the fireplace. 'She seems like a nice, kind lady.' he commented, whilst at the same time trying to imagine his own late mother's persona.

'Who does?' asked the hungry man, busily devouring his heap of steaming hot fish.

'Your mother, in the photograph.'

The gypsy looked up at the picture as well and ceased chewing his food for a moment. 'Aye, the best.' he remarked, whilst inadvertently spraying tiny bits of fish over the table. 'She learned me everyfink I needed to know about life... I loved those years with her, out on the open road with old Toby pulling us.'

'Old Toby?'

'Our horse. Clever old gry him. Crafty too. Wouldn't pull us up an hill until we'd fed him an apple!'

The boy smiled, much amused.

'She was a wise ole bird, my ma. She told me once that the most wonderful thing we possess, save our freedom, is our freedom to roam...And I ain't never forgotten it. Didn't do much travelling in the winters though. Instead, we used to find us a cushti atchin tan somewhere and scratch a living out of the scrap metal. And when times were really hard I knew how to cadge a few smokes out of the gorgers and how to make a few bob, selling the lucky heather.'

The boy listened attentively, fascinated to learn about some of the Romany ways.

'Ah, but the summer times were better boy.' Continued the gypsy, smiling nostalgically. 'It were all picking. We must have worked a hundred farms or more, me an ole ma. All over the southern counties we roamed, as free as the wind and with nothing to our name except the good times ahead of us...She learned me how to skin a bunny and how to bake an hedgehog in the clay.'

The boy grimaced in disgust at the thought of eating such a thing.

'Aye, it were cushti boy! Don't know what you've missed… Anyway, the point is I now know how to cook lots of different things, apple pie an all. And how to properly clean my nashers afterwards. We use the cold ashes, out of the yog. Here, dik at this set o'grinders.' He said, before expanding his jaw wide open and exposing all of his teeth. 'Just like rows of pearls, ain't they boy?'

Chapter 23

It was a perfect evening for a casual stroll upstream along the elevated hillocks, hugging the incoming tide gently rising and hardly noticeable. Low above the horizon thinning cloud cradled the blood-red fireball of the setting sun. The boy gazed up in awe at the evening sky. The effect was almost frightening like Dante's inferno risen from hell. Save an occasional swarm of midges accompanied by one or two bothersome mosquitoes, everywhere was calm. Wildlife silent but watchful. Dykes, ditches and ponds stagnant and the great reed bed dormant and motionless. A sluggish peace had settled upon the marshes.

About a half hour into their ramble, after climbing over the last stile, they came by the travellers' settlement. Unlike the potdigger's home, these gypsies lived in the more modern aluminium caravans shaped like half-moons, about twenty in all. Parked up beside some of them were their trucks fully laden with scrap metal. Jam-packed and piled high with bits of old iron girder, broken car parts and wheel hubs, clapped out radio sets, copper water boilers, clothes mangles and odd pieces of steel and loose wiring. On the ground there were indiscriminate scorch marks of recent fires and scattered here and there were empty propane gas bottles, busted bicycle frames, inoperative kid's toys and several defunct vehicle tyres. An air of poverty hovered over the encampment. Yet, if one was to observe more closely there was wealth too, stealth and undisclosed.

The gypsies went about their business oblivious to the strangers in their midst. Slowly passing by the boy concentrated on all the commotion. The Romany men were stood around in small groups, smoking cigarettes and arguing amongst themselves. Their shawled womenfolk gathering in the washing or attending to their babies. There were a couple of black and white cob horses, their manes long and wild, grazing in an open central area tethered to metal stakes hammered into the ground. A few younger members of the community with mucky faces were happily leading round a patchy brown and white pony, whilst other excited children ran to and fro with their pet dogs loose, playing games with sticks and kicking litter.

When the man and the boy had all but passed by, the gypsies' hounds suddenly got wind of them and began barking wildly. An elderly Romany woman then happened to register who the man was on the hillock. Soon after there followed a great fuss with the mothers crossing themselves and calling out to their children and husbands, summoning them home and locking their caravan doors as if they were in the shadow of the Devil himself.

The boy peered up at his friend and tried to figure out exactly what it was that the gypsies were so afraid of. Not a moment ago the whole site was literally a hive of activity. Now, save for the canine's growling, it was as silent and still as the rest of the marsh. However, the more spirited men among the clan remained out in the open and stood defiantly beside their property. Some of them had drawn their daggers, subtly threatening and gawping up at the maverick with hatred in their hearts. Nevertheless, they sought no trouble from their banished compatriot and were satisfied just to see him on his way.

Ignoring the travellers' contempt they continued on towards the floodgates located up at the head of the creek near where the houseboats were permanently moored. They strolled by the tall asbestos sheds where the big concrete pipes were manufactured and along by Mr Bacon's lemonade factory, lying in the great shadow of the gaswork's gasometer. Just beyond the water barrier, lying flat on the silvery mud, was the little boat which the man had mentioned earlier at the coal jetty. The boy leapt with joy and almost begged the man to hasten his stride along the paper mill's steam pipes upon which they were now treading. He'd noticed that the gypsy was never in a hurry. Everything he did was done slowly, like he had all the time in the world.

Suddenly their progress was thwarted by some mysterious object, lumpy and ragged, lying wedged between the pipes.

'Hang about, who have we here then?' sniggered the gypsy, surprised to discover an old codger who was fast asleep, purring contentedly. Discarded next to him were a couple of empty cider bottles.

The boy had recognised the guy's long white beard. 'It's the tramp from the village…I don't think the poor old man has anywhere to live.'

Many a cold, dark winter had come and gone since Rodger the dodger had first joined that league of gentlemen of the road. They stared down pityingly at the sad bundle of old rags and wondered what cruel tragedy had befallen him all those years ago.

'We better not disturb him then,' suggested the gypsy, taking great care not to wake him as he stepped over his bulky frame. When the boy did likewise he noticed his cockle-hearted friend slip a few pound notes into the old chap's coat pocket.

As they crossed over the floodgates and approached the mini dock the boy's heart sank with disappointment. The vessel seemed in such a dilapidated state, its paintwork almost peeled away. He wasn't sure if he should laugh or cry, 'Oh Tom,' he sighed. It saddened him deeply and put him in mind of an injured soldier returned from the wars, broken and all but done in. On closer inspection he also discovered the mast to be partly missing and the holes that the man had spoken of were a lot worse than he'd imagined.

The gypsy began to kick and poke and pull on the craft. 'Well, she's sound enough up at this pointed end.' he declared. 'Shouldn't be too bad a job getting her done up… What do you reckon?'

The boy wasn't entirely convinced and was inclined to think it beyond repair. Studying it further he found it impossible to emulate the man's optimism and sighed once more.

Sensing the boy's negativity the man then said, 'Cheer up young'n, we'll soon have her fixed up. It ain't that bad… I'll take you down the timber yard next week and then maybe we can make a start.'

Staring at it, the boy slowly began to come round to the idea. 'Can we really, Tom?'

'Of course we will,' promised the jovial gypsy. 'Once upon a time this must have been the finest boat anywhere on the creek and mark my words she can be that again!'

Again the boy felt the need to express his love and

adoration for this man who'd already twice saved his life. He latched onto his side and squeezed him as tight as he could. 'Thank you Tom, you're the best friend anyone could ever have.'

Chapter 24

The boy's bed for the night turned out to be nothing more complex than a small canvas sheet, suspended directly beneath the vardo's wooden floor by short lengths of rope fastened at each of the corners. At first, before he'd got used to the idea, he felt much like a fruit bat hanging in the dark. However, he had to admit that in addition to the soft feather pillow and the thick cozy blanket the man had lent him it was perfectly snug. He wasn't that bothered about the fact that he was now sleeping outside. Or about the loud rasping noise coming from above. Having only ever slept in the boy's dormitory he was used to the sounds of snoring. In any case he wasn't the least bit tired. Right now his mind was preoccupied with thoughts of the little boat and he was excited at the prospect of restoring it. But his faith in the man's ability to achieve this objective remained doubtful and as things stood it was more a case of hope than confidence.

Suddenly the boy cried out in pain, 'Aargh!'

The thud from under the floor had jolted the man up out of his sleep and then wondering what all the kerfuffle was about he shouted down to his young guest. 'You all right, boy?'

The boy was still wincing in pain. He'd felt something beneath the tarpaulin prod his lower back causing him to wallop his head on the underside of the caravan.

Following a short spell of uncertainty the man repeated his question.

'Yeah, I think so,' replied the boy.

'What do you mean you think so, what have you done?'

'Nothing, I just accidently banged my head…but I don't think it's bleeding.'

'Are you sure you're all right then?'

'Yes, I'm all right now.' He was nursing a small bump which had formed on his forehead.

'Be careful under there.'

'I will, goodnight.'

'Aye lad, go to sleep now.'

A short while later, when he was sure that the man had nodded off again, he squeezed his head out through the gap at the edge of his bed. Beyond the tarpaulin he could see quite clearly bathed in the moonlight a beautiful red vixen. The guilty party, he presumed. He also thought it might be the same fox he'd been shown earlier. She was foraging around for scraps of food. Scratching the ground and sniffing the air she suddenly picked up the boy's scent and came closer to investigate.

'Hello Mrs Fox,' he whispered, staring into its glassy eyes which glowed like hot coals. 'And how are you this fine evening?'

The slightly nervous animal padded a few steps in reverse before it turned about completely and raced off empty bellied in the direction of its den.

Chapter 25

The following morning, at around nine o'clock, Mrs Saffron decided to ring the boy up at his friend's house, Christopher Crispin's. Bearing in mind the jackdaw's sudden decline in its general wellbeing, she'd thought it best to tell him to come home straight away. However, when Mr Crispin said he hadn't seen the boy for some weeks, Mrs Saffron almost dropped the telephone receiver in distress. 'Are you quite certain?' she asked, extremely alarmed. 'He assured us both that he was staying with your son and it was all arranged.'

Whilst remaining on the line, the undertaker called out for young Christopher just to make sure that he hadn't got it wrong.

'No papa,' confirmed the apple of his father's eye. 'I haven't seen Tommy since last week at school when he borrowed my compass and magnifying glass,' he said, before adding rather sulkingly, 'And he hasn't given them back to me yet!'

Having overheard their conversation, Mrs Saffron suddenly felt faint and was forced to sit down. 'Umm, OK then Mr Crispin, I'm sorry to have bothered you.'

'Not at all, not at all… But is there a problem then, Mrs Saffron?'

'No, no. I've obviously got it all muddled up. He must have meant one of his other friends,' she returned, very much doubting her own supposition. 'But please, if either of you do happen to see him, would you ask him to come home straight away?'

'Yes of course we will, Mrs Saffron.'

'Well cheerio then, Mr Crispin.' She replaced the telephone receiver temporarily before picking it up again and dialing 999.

Chapter 26

About twenty minutes after Mrs Saffron had telephoned the emergency services, a blue Ford Anglia patrol car pulled up sharply at the curbside directly outside of Greenporch. Two uniformed officers stepped out of the police vehicle and greeted the anxious woman already waiting for them at the front gate. Trying his best to calm his frantic wife, Mr Saffron promptly ushered them all inside.

'Now then madam,' began the ruddy-faced sergeant, 'could you please give us a brief description of the missing child. A recent snapshot would be helpful.' The younger constable pulled out his notebook and pencil from his top pocket and stood ready to jot down all of the particulars. The tearful women, holding a crumpled handkerchief up to her face, then proceeded to explain about her telephone call earlier to Mr Crispin.

'So in actual fact then, the boy's been absent since early Saturday morning. Is that correct?'

Rather sheepishly, the boy's legal guardians both nodded in confirmation.

The sergeant then added, reassuringly, 'That's assuming of course that he hadn't changed his mind and went to stay with another of his friends instead. Which I might add usually turns out to be the case.'

Mrs Saffron blew her nose and dried her eyes. 'After I'd called you I sent the twins, that's Veronica and Daisy – our eldest, round to check on his other friends. Nugger, Ernie and Johnny. They're all the same age as Tommy and live just over there on the estate… neither of the boys have laid eyes on him. And sometimes he plays with Jimmy up in the coal yard but I've already phoned his mum.'

'With respect, missus,' explained the younger policeman, 'we'll still require their addresses, just to be on the safe side. They may well have spun the girls a bit of a yarn, boys being boys.'

'Yes, I suppose so,' agreed Mrs Saffron, in submission. 'Oh, I'm such a fool, I should have made sure!' She kept on repeating this over and over again. Chastising herself for foolishly allowing the boy to pull the wool over her eyes.

'You see, sergeant,' interposed her husband, handing the policeman one of the boy's school photographs. 'We've never had occasion to doubt his integrity. As far as we were aware, Tommy was meant to be staying up at the undertaker's place.'

'Yes I see,' said the sergeant, staring down at the boy's image. 'Before I organise a search, I'd like to take a quick look through the boy's personal effects if I may. His school books, diary, et cetera. They may well provide us with some clue to his present whereabouts.'

The policemen were then escorted to the boy's dormitory where they hurriedly began to snoop among his personal belongings. 'We also need to establish what the lad was wearing,' continued the sergeant, 'and whether or not he's taken any spare clothing with him.'

Mrs Saffron then anxiously began to rummage through the boy's remaining clothes hanging up in his wardrobe.

Meanwhile, stood at the corner of the cul-de-sac waiting for the bus to Sittingbourne and observing all of the goings on, was the dreaded Bertha Musgrave. Renowned for her poisonous tittle-tattle, she was unashamedly the current owner of the largest of the many wooden spoons constantly stirring in the village. To her many victims, whose lives and reputations she has so wilfully destroyed, she remains the epitome of evil.

She seldom visited her husbands' grave, having felt no obligation to do so, but today was one of those rare occasions when she was pleased she had, albeit very briefly. Ruled by her insatiable nosiness and forgoing her trip to the shops, she plodded up and down the pavement tutting with impatience until the policemen finally re-emerged. They were accompanied by the Saffrons whom looked terribly worried, a very tearful Mrs Stickles, in her white pinny, her dumbstruck husband and most of the excited children whom lived there as well.

Desperate to find out exactly what was going on, she seized upon her one chance to eavesdrop and proceeding by the gateway at a snail's pace managed to ascertain a few snippets of the unfolding drama. She'd also noticed that one of the police officers was holding what looked suspiciously like a boy's t-shirt. Busting a gut to relay her new tidings to whomever was prepared to listen, Bertha Musgrave rushed off back up the hill to the village proper, filling in herself the bits of their conversations which she hadn't quite grasped. Unbeknown to the two police officers and everyone else concerned all hell was about to break loose!

Chapter 27

After he'd slackened the tie ropes like the man had already demonstrated, the boy was easily able to escape his bed, greeting the new day with a good, long stretch. He'd benefitted from a full night's sleep, dreamless and rejuvenating and had high hopes of his next adventure upon the marshes. Overhead there was a thin ceiling of rippled cloud, low and motionless. The morning was dense with silence and everywhere was still except for a sudden invasion of a multitude of cabbage white butterflies. He watched them fluttering with life, dancing spontaneously and finally settling as gracefully as gently falling snowflakes. Inhaling the wholesome sea air he was again affected by a strange sense of attachment. He felt an affiliation with the place as if he'd always belonged here.

There was something weird and wonderful about this washback, he realised. Cut off and somehow insulated from the rest of the world and all of its troubles, it seemed to him to glow in a different light. A separate, paradoxical environment almost, that contained a special peace and calmness of its own, one which he felt he could almost reach out and touch. Whatever it was he knew that he never wanted to leave it and was beginning to appreciate why the recluse had chosen this alternative lifestyle. Here in the wilderness there existed no fear or sadness. Here there was only life.

But something was wrong. It was just *too* quiet. Cautiously he climbed the steps up into the vardo and stood hesitantly between the doorframes. He wasn't sure why but he was not the least bit surprised to find it empty, having felt like he'd stepped aboard a ghost ship that had suddenly been forsaken in a dried up sea.

Everything was out of place and incongruous, the air inside heavy with abandonment. The gypsy's bed was unmade and nothing had been tidied away. A greasy frying pan had been left on the side of the stove. Dirty plates, cups and cutlery were piled high in the washing up bowl. The floor was messy and unswept and left behind on the draining board was the man's pipe and tobacco pouch.

Amid the chaos however, the boy noticed a folded sheet of writing paper lying on the sideboard. On it was scribbled a note which read; 'HALP YOR SALF TO SUM GRUB BOY. I BE BACK LATA.' He rubbed his sore head and was pleased that his bump had all but disappeared. He sat down at the man's table and poured himself a bowl of cereal. Gazing out of the window he was content to sit quietly and wait for his return.

Chapter 28

Bertha Musgrave had maintained her furious pace all the way up from Greenporch Close and by the time she'd reached the high street on the crown of the hill, she was bent at right angles and gasping for breath.

Towering above everyone else in the queue outside of Milton post office was one of her closest cronies and gossip buddy, Mrs Dorothy Smith. The woman was so thin she looked like a match with the wood scraped off.

'All Gawd blimey, whatever's the matter?' she cried, fussing around her friend like an old mother hen.

Holding a hand up to her heaving bosom and struggling to breathe, Bertha M replied, 'Oh, give us a minute Dot, will you...Just while I catch my breath.'

'But are you sure you're all right, dear?'

'In a moment Dot, I just need a bit of a breather.' Wheezed Bertha M. Her large muscular tongue, aching to spill the beans but not yet able to communicate properly. She had a face much like a bulldog's, chewing a wasp.

Dorothy Smith bit her lip and fidgeted with impatience. To be perfectly frank not a lot had happened around the village of late and so she was determined to enjoy this one.

Whatever it was that her friend was so desperate to tell her she knew it was bound to be good. But most annoyingly she had to endure another minute or so of the agonising silence before the exhausted women was finally able to speak.

'Well Dot,' began Bertha M, her lips had now formed into a conceited smirk. 'He's finally gone and done it!'

'Who has?' fired back the engrossed Mrs Smith.

'Him!'

'Him?... him who?'

'Him what roams the marshes, Blackberry Bill, that's who!'

'Good gracious me, not him.'

'Saw it all with my own eyes Dot. Strike me down dead if I didn't!'

'Oh my word Bee, what's he done then?'

'A dozen or so coppers I counted.'

'Oh no, where?'

'Down that children's home, that's where!'

'Heavens above, not the little ones.'

Bertha Musgrave raised her brow and nodded in disgust.

'No, please don't tell me it's the kids, Berth.'

'It's my poor old Albert I worry about, Dot. Never a moment's peace. Him long in his grave and all. I shouldn't wonder if he isn't turning in it right this very moment knowing what I know.'

'When was all this then?' asked Dorothy S, becoming more frustrated with every passing second, knowing full well that she'd missed out on something colossal.

'Not a quarter of an hour ago.' Bertha M replied, gloating with glee. 'But haven't I always said it, Dot? Haven't I always made it known? Wasn't I right to say it?'

Her friend's head was bobbing up and down like a punkahwallah's arm at the hottest hour of the day.

'I knew he was a bad sort, that old Blackberry. I knew he'd do something like this, Dot.'

'Bee, he hasn't…'

'He has, he's gone and stolen one of the young urchins from the orphanage.'

'Oh God no!' gasped her friend, cupping her mouth with the palm of her hand.

'A young boy, apparently.'

'How awful!'

'I clocked one of those coppers clutching an item of his clothing.'

'I dare say that'll be for the sniffer dogs, Berth.' Said the beanpole.

'Exactly!'

'Oh, that poor child.'

Bertha Musgrave's wicked assumption had sparked into reality and now burned its course down the line of earwigging pensioners like a lighted fuse wire on a stick of dynamite.

Chapter 29

The gypsy had eaten his breakfast and was already out on the marshes digging up the pots as was his passion to do so. Earlier it had rained again quite hard and the weather this morning looked much the same as it did yesterday. Sunshine with scattered showers. But at least the rain had softened the dirt, he thought.

Having heard the boy in the night, fidgeting around under the vardo, he'd decided to leave the clearing up to allow his young friend to sleep in and therefore was toiling alone. However, out on the cloudy horizon just before noon something peculiar began to occur. Somewhat baffled, he scratched his head whilst trying to work out what the strange dark shapes were slowly heading towards him. Soon he realised, to his utter consternation, that the black dots in motion were in actual fact people. Hundreds of the locals whom were obviously searching for the boy. He'd been half expecting something like this having already assumed that his young companion had run away from the children's home. Dropping the digging fork, he ran back towards the washbacks in disarray knowing that he had to act fast or else he'd lose the boy forever.

When he'd got back to the caravan, he noticed with much relief that he was already up and dressed. He was sat down in the grass playing with the pots again. 'Quick boy, we've got to leave here now,' he insisted, grabbing hold of the boy firmly by the wrist.

'But why, Tom? Where are we going?'

'Come on now,' implored the gypsy. 'There's somemink else I've got to show you!'

Both were then startled by the sudden maddening presence of a noisy bird which had swooped down out of nowhere and landed on the boy's shoulder.

'Hello Jack, what are you doing here?' The boy stretched out his arm and allowed the bird to walk down to his fingers. 'You crafty devil! How did you know where I was?'

The jackdaw ruffled its black feathers and cawed continuously, seemingly pleased to have found its young master.

'Tom, this is Jack,' said the boy, cheerfully. 'My faithful friend… What do you think of him?'

The gypsy was more concerned about the search party which he knew must be drawing ever closer. 'Aye lad, he's a lively one,' he remarked. 'But boy, it ain't safe here now, we've got to leave.'

'Not safe?'

'I'll explain later. Come on, let's go.'

Chapter 30

The boy then found himself to some extent being frog-marched back towards the orphanage beside the church, both buildings now appearing salient beneath the arch of an awesomely beautiful rainbow. 'Where are you taking me?' he asked, nervous at the thought of returning home so soon. The rain had ceased and the sun was shining behind cumulus clouds and he wanted to play down by the creek.

'Not much farther to go now,' promised the man, stomping along as if he was late for something.

The boy had got it into his head that the gypsy man, for reasons of his own, was about to betray him. He was wholly convinced that the man wasn't going to stop his relentless pace until he'd escorted him right up to the green porchway of the orphanage. 'No I don't want to go home!' he protested, pulling away from the man.

'Look'ere,' began the gypsy. 'Who said anyfink about going home? I just want to show you somemink, like I told you.'

The boy was not yet persuaded and stood hesitating, doubt mingling among his thoughts.

Just then the farmer came trundling along the dirt track

in his brand new Massey Ferguson loading shovel. Farmer Pat was a proud and jolly fellow. The sleeves of his thick cotton lumberjack shirt were rolled up tight against his large biceps and he had a lighted hand-rolled cigarette wedged between his lips. Sat next to him in the cab of the tractor was his dainty little wife 'Micky', puffing on a No 6 cigarette and wearing a contented smile from ear to ear. Sitting in the raised front digging bucket of the noisy machine were their three young children, two fair headed boys and a girl with a mass of ginger curly hair. The children waved to the man and the boy with the bird on his shoulder and were all giggling with excitement, riding high on their dad's new tractor. The gypsy and the runaway returned their smiles and waved back.

The boy clammed up and began to distance himself but the gypsy really had no wish to upset him. In a much softer tone of voice he tried to explain. 'Look, when I saw them words in your bag, l.a.n.g.l.e.y (he pronounced each letter individually such as a young child would do), I knew then that you must be my pipsqueak brother because they're the same words as on me father's gravestone over in that there mulladipoos.'

'Brother?' The boy mouthed the word but it was hardly audible. His jaw dropped and his pupils dilated and he didn't trust his own ears. Had the man really said that?

'Them words, Thomas Edwin Langley, gouged out of that slab. And he's my father right enough, as sure as the sun in the sky and the wind and the sea and these'ere boodiful marshes. My mother swore blind to it and strike her down dead again if it ain't the honest truth!'

As regard to the aforementioned contentious issue, the boy was rendered temporarily speechless. However, he silently agreed to accompany the man and staggering like a zombie with his eyes wet with emotion, he managed to reach as far as the churchyard wall. Here he had to rest a while, trying desperately to make sense out of the inner conflict tearing his mind apart. The discerning gypsy sat down alongside him and kept quiet. Gazing back out admiringly at the wilderness of the marshland he was fully aware that what he'd just disclosed must have shocked the boy. But it was the only way.

Chapter 31

Leaping down from the churchyard wall the man gently took hold of the boy's trembling hand and led him and his jackdaw slowly through the graves over to the great yew tree in the far corner.

Suddenly a wayward gust of wind blew vehemently amongst the tombstones, rustling the leaves, stirring up twigs and dust and whistling its eerie melody as if attempting to wake the dead. Both man and boy squinted and cowered against the blast. The bird squawked and flapped its wings in protest. The gypsy was also peering around uncertainly in all directions as if he was somehow trying to read the omens. But then, as rapidly as it had formed, the freak whirlwind died away allowing the usual peace and calm to resume.

'See there,' said the man, pointing down at the boy's parent's gravestone. 'That's my father's grave,' he confided and once again he respectfully drew the sign of the cross symbolically on his chest.

The boy was still disinclined to believe what he was hearing but following a brief pause then said with a degree of confidence, 'You're the one that always leaves the flowers, aren't you?'

'Aye, it was me whose put a few fresh petals over his grave from time to time…Out of respect like.'

The boy nodded very slowly as if to commend the gypsy's esteem for the parent they'd supposedly had in common.

'Course, I never knew him but he's my father all the same and you've got to show some respect and that for your father, aincher?'

'What's your other name then?'

'What, d'you mean my family name?'

'Yes, what is your surname?'

'Well I'm a Baker, Tommy Baker is me… But what's that got to do with it? It's my mother's maiden name not my father's. You see, I'm a Baker because my ma and pa, God bless'em, never jumped the sticks.' The gypsy finished his explanation by crossing himself.

The boy felt even more confused.

'That means that they'd never got spliced, you know, married like. Anyhow, when I saw them words in your bag,' the man continued, 'they'd set me thinking and I soon put two and two together and I knew then that you must be that sprog what I saved from that horrible yog which killed my father… I spose you'd be about ten now, aincher?'

The boy nodded again.

'I thought you was the lady's baby. Never knew she was married to me dad…not until I got out of hospital.'

The boy flopped to his knees beside the grave and tried to digest all of what his brain was consuming. The bird hopped over onto the headstone that he knew so well and settled down for another of the long waits he'd grown accustomed to.

The man knelt down next to the boy. 'Course, my father never knew he had a nipper in tow because my mother never told him. Somemink to do with her Romany pride and honour and that, I dunno. They were both young fools, she said. As stubborn as mules. She'd refused to give up her travellers' life and likewise my dad couldn't let go of the sea. So eventually they drifted apart and went their own separate ways…But they'd loved each other though and she told me, like it or not, that I was the living proof of their love… When I was growing up though, I never knew anything about him, not even his name. Can't imagine why but my mother had never uttered a word of his being. Not until she was almost at death's door, did she suddenly change her mind and blurt out everything that she thought I needed to know. And of course, she told me where I could find my father after she'd died and gone up there,' he said, looking up at the clouds.

Dumbfounded, the boy struggled to accept these revelations. For as long as he cared to remember he'd always yearned to be part of a real family. Now, suddenly and according to the gypsy, it would seem that he has his very own half-brother who happens to be none other than Blackberry Bill, the infamous nomad of the marshes and the mysterious man that every other Miltonian was afraid of.

'What happened to your mother?' asked the boy, consciously beginning to accept the fact that they shared the same father. Indeed there were no physical similarities between the two of them whatsoever but through their veins flowed the old sea dog's blood. His lost sons, finally united by an innocent hand of fate.

'Died, God bless'er heart,' the man replied, crossing himself. 'Ten years back…consumption. We lived over near Tenterden way in those days…you know, for the fruit picking and that like I told you, ankas n'gurlos mostly.'

'So after your mother had sadly passed away, you came here to Milton Regis?' Asked the boy, now desperately wanting to believe it all as the unequivocal truth.

'Yep, me and our horse Toby and my mother's vardo. We all came here looking for my father, the only family I thought I had left.'

The boy held back his question for a moment trying to summon up the courage to ask, 'Did…did you actually meet my father then, I mean our father?'

Before answering this the gypsy smiled to himself knowing that the boy had finally begun to acknowledge him as his sibling. 'Nope, like I said he never knew me … I didn't even get the chance to see him. I'd only come here a divvus before the fire. I didn't even realise it was my father's boat gone up in smoke. Not until I was all better and out of hospital. Course, I had to tell'em to sell Toby, my gry, otherwise he would've died too….of starvation.'

Turmoil and frustration had somehow changed into clarity and calm. The boy was beginning to understand and now listened more attentively.

'I'd lain flat on my back with about as much strength as a kitten for almost a year, having one operation after the other in that East Grinstead hospital and when the doctors finally got me fixed up I came back here the following winter to claim my property.'

'Do you mean your caravan, Tom?'

'Aye, and all my mother's things she'd left me. Except when I got here I reckoned on a staying a while because I didn't have Toby anymore and it's a cushti atchin tan as anywhere…And besides, I'd nowhere else to go anyway.

Like I said, I ain't got no one left on my mother's side because all that lot are now dead and buried in the mulladipoos. Anyhow, at the time, I still thought my father was alive and well somewhere and I had every intention of finding him. But shortly after I'd got back'ere, this swanky looking gadgie turned up out of nowhere - all suited and booted, he was. He said he was from the Gazette and that they wanted to do a follow-up story or somemink about that terrible night. Straight away he pounced on my case trying to wangle things out of me. Course, I just let him babble on, all the time asking questions…Fair do's, he seemed a decent sort I spose but I'd got it in my head to keep schtum. The last thing I needed was for my present whereabouts to be plastered all over the front page of the local rag. It would've been like waving a red flag in front of every stroppy gorger in the town. So of course, I kept my trap shut and in the death he got fed up with me…Before the mush cleared off altogether though, he was kind enough to leave me some copies of the old newspapers.'

The boy looked at the man somewhat furtively, now reminded of the scrapbook, he'd secretly read yesterday.

'You see,' pursued the gypsy, 'this was when I first learnt the names of the barge folks that'd died in the fire that winter afore. It near on knocked me off my feet when I read that it was my own father and his wife who'd been killed - our poor ole dad here and your dear, sweet mother.' The gypsy crossed himself twice and the boy copied him.

'I promised him though, in my prayers,' he continued, sparing the tearful boy the cruel truth of those wretched days succeeding the reporter's visit, when he'd lain suffering on his bed, brokenhearted, sobbing with grief and haunted by the recurring nightmare of his father's premature death.

'I swore him an oath that I wouldn't rest until I'd found his flesh and blood, his and mine!'

The boy was struggling to contain all of his pent-up emotion.

'Trouble was, I never knew which kid's home the nurse had whisked you off to, or who I could ask to find out... But, as God's me judge boy, I must've banged on the door of every one of 'em this side of the Medway, including that place there!' he explained, pointing a little resentfully at the Greenporch orphanage. 'And d'you know what, everywhere I went, I was either swore at, spat at, or forcibly turned on my heels and sent packing by the gorgers...After a while I began to wonder, what was the point of it all? It seemed to me that nobody was interested in what I'd got to say. Even if I had found you, they wasn't going to let me see you. I'd wasted month after month roaming here, there and everywhere, in all weathers too, searching for you. Then one day, and it pains me to say it boy, when I was soaking wet, tired out and burning up with fever, I had to beg my broken heart to finally let you go...But I'll tell you this young'n, as I kneel here before this house of the Lord's, that it never once crossed my mind that you might only be a stone's throw away all the while. I just thought I was on my own again.'

The boy stared into the man's dark eyes. 'You saved me when I was a baby,' he said, with a deep emotion beginning to constrict his windpipe.

'Aye, it was me boy who done it. When I saw them flames raging I knew it must be one of those barges on the creek. So I ran down to it faster than old Toby and I saw this bargeman and his woman trying their hardest to dowse it out with buckets of water. It's still down there that barge, what little's left of it, alongside that rusty old tug.'

'What did they look like?' asked the boy, aching to learn any slightest detail of his parent's features but shivering at the thought that he'd already stepped among the charred remains of their former home and livelihood.

'Who?'

'The bargeman and the woman!' retorted the boy, unable to prevent himself from feeling just a little bit jealous. 'My mother and father.'

'Didn't much notice. Excepting the light from the fire it was awfully del and of course I never knew it was my father at the time. Everyfink happened so fast, next minute I knew they were gone. The decking seemed to collapse directly under their feet... The poor souls didn't have a chance.'

Listening to his brother's harrowing account of what had actually occurred on that tragic night, the boy felt a great knot tighten in his stomach and tears stinging the corners of his wide eyes.

'That's when I heard this baby screaming its head off. They'd put you safe boy, up at the end of the boat, away from the flames. All wrapped up in a cosy white blanket you was, snuggled up in a bushel box...Then I saw them flames jumping and roaring and spreading fast, with the wind you see...and I only just managed to get you off in time, thank God...Funny that though, you being my baby brother all along and I never knew it.'

Now the boy was weeping quietly.

'That's why I've got all these burns,' explained the man, before standing upright and unbuttoning his shirt, revealing the full extent of his awful injuries. The plain fact was that he was still only a man in his late twenties but his scarring had aged him terribly. Even so, he carried a wise head on his young shoulders. 'Yucky blighters, ain't they?' he added, vivaciously.

Sympathetically, the boy studied the skin on the man's neck and chest and it looked to him as though it had partly melted away. Twisted, ugly, yellow and purple scars. Such an unjust reward for a truly brave act of humanity which has cost him dearly. He much pitied his elder sibling and stricken with a gut wrenching sense of guilt, wished he too had croaked along with his parents so as to waiver his poor brother's sufferance. In his young heart there was one thing more precious than life and that was love itself.

He was humbled by what he'd been shown but his illegitimate gypsy brother seemed almost proud of his disfigurements, as if they were the wounds of battle inflicted by the enemy in an heroic war. And not once had he heard this modest man complain of his crosses to bear. Nor did he seem bitter or sad with regard to the prejudiced treatment he'd received year after year from the local populace. Even his own kind had felt fit to ostracize him. The boy bowed his head in shame.

Watching him fussing over the grave, the boy then understood that it must have been his brother who had bought his parent's beautiful headstone. Paid for through years of sweat and toil digging up the pots. And he'd done this deed alone, thought the boy, out of love and respect for the father he'd been deprived of. The father, both of them had never known.

Chapter 32

Both the man and the boy were conscious of the fact that they were no longer alone. In actual fact it now appeared that half the townsfolk had turned out to join in the search for the missing boy and were now lining the graveyard's perimeter, effectively entrapping them. Some were sitting on the churchyard wall itself whilst others peered over it. The news of the so called kidnapping had spread like wildfire, especially when one busy old blabbermouth now skulking amongst the crowd had ignited a malicious rumour that the loner, Blackberry Bill, had abducted the child.

'There's the culprit!' cried one of the scores of angry faces. 'Come on then lads, let's get him!' bawled another. Through the grapevine, it'd become apparent to the volatile mob, whom were now ready to lynch the gypsy with their coshes and batons held aloft, that the captive had somehow escaped his brutal abductor who in turn had chased him here. They were all positively seething and collectively baying for the man's blood with exception of the paranoid schizophrenic gravedigger. Apart from feeling narked and somewhat put out by all of the intrusive company, old Joseph Crow couldn't have cared less and continued working like a navvy to finish his hole before the pubs closed.

Stood under the church lychgate at the spearhead of this upheaval were the boy's legal guardians, along with a number of officers from the local constabulary whom now believed the gyspy to be highly dangerous. Mr and Mrs Saffron, desperately wishing to protect and comfort their ward, had to be restrained by force. A German Shepherd, held firm on a short leash, had been unmuzzled and was barking continuously. Amid escalating jeers and insults from the belligerent crowd the inspector in charge, intent on apprehending the fiend, finally began to speak through his loudhailer. 'I CALL UPON YOU THERE, THE PERSON KNOWN FOR ALL INTENTS AND PURPOSES AS BLACKBERRY BILL, TO STEP AWAY FROM THAT CHILD AND TO GIVE YOURSELF UP FREELY… TO ATTEMPT ESCAPE WOULD BE FUTILE. YOU ARE COMPLETELY SURROUNDED!'

The gypsy wasn't the least bit concerned but the boy became very upset by the policeman's demands. He screamed out at the approaching throng. 'But you don't understand. He's not going to hurt me, he saved my life. This is my brother and I love him!'

The boy then looked up at his saviour and noticed a tear trickle down the side of his crooked, purple face. He could do nothing more than sob his heart out as he affectionately embraced his courageous, loving brother.

Gasps of shock and disbelief and from some even cries of disappointment, reverberated around the mass of onlookers, most of which then soon began to disperse.

'That's our father,' said the gypsy proudly, fighting back

his own tears. 'Lying alongside your mother… And you're my little brother. And now you're my family.'

Chapter 33

The Norfolk coast, the year 2000.

Tom Langley stared aimlessly up at the ceiling, his mind still searching among the remnants of his childhood memories. He'd already rooted out and relived a great deal of those precious moments he'd spent with his gypsy brother. The hot summers when they'd swam together in the creek or in the pond on the mysterious, colourful island. He thought of their many fishing trips and the fish they'd caught. All of the different animals they'd cared for on the marshes and those intriguing pots and bottles, like buried treasure, they'd dug up out of the ground. And he remembered especially those times when they'd laughed and cried together.

The fact that they shared their father's Christian name was merely a coincidence but he'd been thinking about the other Tom a lot these past few days and of those strange marshes where they'd miraculously found each other. In the intervening years since that memorable day in the churchyard, when the police had arrested his brother for his own protection and subsequently released him without charge, they'd remained very close.

Tom was now an affluent designer of luxurious yachts for the super rich, having gradually worked his way up through the lucrative industry from the humble beginnings of an apprentice Boatwright. He put the success of his career mainly down to his brother's continued love and support and not least his shrewdness in matters of finance. He felt that he owed him everything.

Contrary to his Romany tradition and despite his younger brother's immense wealth, the sagacious gypsy had always refused to abandon his frugal but happy life on the marshes. He'd kept his promise though and repaired that little boat in which Tom had learnt to sail on Milton Creek. As a boy he'd proudly named her *'The Potdigger'*, hand painting the letters himself and then many years later, when he could well afford his own private yacht, again he'd named her after his eccentric brother before setting off from the Isle of Wight and sailing her around the globe.

He'd fled here to this run-down B&B beside the sea, with its broken tap, moth-eaten curtains and wonky old bed, simply because it was as far away as he'd wanted to run. But it is somewhere he has come to appreciate. A vast, lonely shore along which he's allowed himself to grieve. To weep. And to remember. Three days ago he'd been respectfully informed that his brother, better known as Blackberry Bill, had passed away. He was fifty-nine years old and he died alone but peacefully in his mother's vardo upon those marshes beloved to them both.

Tom got up and reached for his bag. There was nothing else he could do other than to accept what had happened. The funeral is tomorrow and so now he must leave. After attending to his bill he stepped outside and stood on the veranda for a moment, filling his lungs with the fresh air blowing down from across the North Sea. Before getting into his car he took one last affectionate look at the deserted dunes of the sweeping bay.

Finally, he turned the key to the ignition and somewhat apprehensively drove his way back to the Milton marshes.

THE END

Glossary

Romany	English
ankas	pears
atchin tan	stopping-place
chavvie	gyspy child
cushti	good
del	dark
dik	look
dinlo	fool
divvus	day
divvy	stupid
gadgie	non gypsy man
gorger	non gypsy person
gry	horse
gurlos	cherries
jel	go
mulladipoos	graveyard
mush	man
simmin	soup
vardo	caravan
wafti	bad
wongur	money
yog	fire
yok	eye

Acknowledgments

I'd like to offer my most sincere gratitude to my agent and editor, James Essinger, for his belief in me; his professionalism and his invaluable advice.

My heartfelt thanks also for their kind assistance to my late mother, Patricia 'Micky' Reardon, George and Marjorie Broomfield, Christine Melloy, Jack Shilling and the staff at the Old Court Hall Museum.

Special thanks to my dear friend Sarah Heathfield for her lasting patience, dedication and hard work in typing up the manuscript, and to Charlotte Mouncey for the cover design and the typesetting.

Above all, a great big thank-you to my lovely wife Judy for all her help and for encouraging me to finish the book.

By the same author
Bay of Dreams (The Conrad Press, 2019)

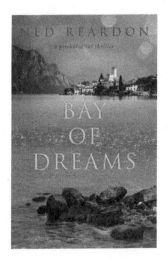

There is a Facebook Page available for *Bay of Dreams*
that contains further information